THE P...
By J...

Opposites attract...
and a by-the-book...
everything. Can there be a happily-ever-after
if two feisty young people believe compromise
is a dirty word, and are determined to ignore
the attraction that sizzles between them?

Kimani Romance is Proud to Present

THREE WEDDINGS & A REUNION

THE LOCKHARTS—
Three Weddings and a Reunion
For four sassy sisters, romance changes everything!

* * *

And don't miss baby sister's high jinks
in the next episodes of

THE LOCKHARTS—
Three Weddings and a Reunion

HIS HOLIDAY BRIDE
by Elaine Overton
October 2007

FORBIDDEN TEMPTATION
by Gwynne Forster
November 2007

Available from Kimani Romance!

Books by Jacquelin Thomas

Kimani Romance
The Pastor's Woman

Kimani New Spirit

Saved in the City
Soul Journey
Change is Gonna Come
The Prodigal Husband

Kimani Arabesque

Treasures of the Heart
To Mom, with Love
"The Price of a Mother's Love"
Stolen Hearts
With a Song in My Heart
Undeniably Yours
Love's Miracle
Family Ties
Cupid's Arrow
"Heart to Heart"
Someone Like You
Forever Always
Hidden Blessings

JACQUELIN THOMAS's

love for romance was born out of sneaking into her mother's room in search of a good book. She was thirteen at the time, and from that moment on, she would read everything from historical to contemporary romances. When she decided to try her hand at writing, the romance genre was a natural choice for her. Jacquelin is the author of more than thirty titles, and is currently at work on her next project.

Jacquelin THOMAS

The Pastor's Woman

KIMANI
ROMANCE

 KIMANI PRESS™

ISBN-13: 978-0-373-86032-6
ISBN-10:   0-373-86032-3

THE PASTOR'S WOMAN

Copyright © 2007 by Harlequin Books S.A.

www.kimanipress.com

Printed in U.S.A.

Dear Reader,

We all make mistakes. Have you ever wished you'd been born with a reset button, or the ability to set the clock back to before a mistake occurred?

Forgiving ourselves is as close as we come to a reset button. So why is it the hardest thing to do?

This is the question that plagues Wade Kendrick in *The Pastor's Woman*. A man with a troubled past, Wade preaches forgiveness, but finds his faith lacking when it comes to facing his personal demons.

The Pastor's Woman is the second book in THE LOCKHARTS—THREE WEDDINGS AND A REUNION, a series featuring four sisters. This book is about Pearl Lockhart, the quintessential middle sister and an aspiring gospel singer. Pearl enjoys living life to the fullest. In contrast, Wade is a much more traditional guy. Their relationship begins with a rocky start because Pearl and Wade disagree on just about everything, from music and fashion to the roles of women in the household. And yet they soon discover that opposites attract when it comes to love.

I truly enjoyed writing this story, and fell in love with Pearl's ability to stand firm in her beliefs and with her courage to stay the course in making her dreams come true.

I hope you enjoy reading it.

Jacquelin

This book is dedicated to the loves of my life:
My husband and my children. Forever always…

Chapter 1

The dark clouds looming ominously over Detroit, the thirty-four-degree temperature and thirty-five-mile-per-hour winds matched Pearl Lockhart's mood perfectly as she merged her Ford Explorer onto I-75 north on her way to Lakeview Baptist Church.

She left fifteen minutes early because she wanted to have a few words with the pastor. Just who did Wade Kendrick think he was, telling her that she should wear her dresses a little longer? What nerve!

The man had only been installed a few months

ago as pastor of the church she grew up in, and now he was suddenly an authority on fashion.

Her sisters had invited Pastor Wade Kendrick to attend their annual family reunion last month and he seemed nice enough—until he made a chauvinistic comment regarding the roles of women in a Christian household, igniting a heated debate between him and Pearl.

He had a lot of nerve criticizing the way she dressed. God didn't care about the clothes people wore to church. He looked at the heart and not the garments. It wasn't as if she were walking into church dressed like a hoochie. Her skirts normally reached just above the knee. For goodness' sake, she was only twenty-five years old.

Pearl pulled her SUV into the church parking lot that sat on the corner of Monroe Street.

She climbed out a few minutes later, braving the November chill. Pearl pulled together the folds of her ankle-length leather coat and walked briskly toward the entrance of the church. She loved the city of her birth, but during this time of year, she developed a love-hate relationship with the Michigan weather.

Pearl moved easily but impatiently through the wooden double doors of Lakeview Baptist

Church. "Good morning," she said to one of the deacons standing outside the sanctuary. Removing her coat, she headed down the hallway to the administrative offices.

She was relieved that none of her sisters had arrived yet, especially Ruby or Opal. They would try to talk her out of her plan, but Pearl had never been one to back down from a fight.

When she neared Wade's office, Pearl slowed her pace. The door was slightly ajar, allowing her to peek inside.

He was there, his bald head gleaming as he concentrated on the papers on his mahogany desk. Pearl had to admit that Wade was a handsome man with dark brown eyes and nice full lips. Even that secret expression she'd glimpsed from time to time made him sexy.

She'd heard through the church grapevine that he was only twenty-eight years old, despite his somber mood and old-fashioned attitude.

She knocked softly to get his attention.

Without waiting for a response, Pearl pushed the door open all the way and struck a pose. "So what do you think of this outfit, Pastor? Does it meet with your approval?"

Wade Kendrick eyed the petite woman standing in the doorway of his office wearing a black leather skirt that was cut a good two inches above the knee revealing shapely, well-toned legs.

His left eyebrow rose up a fraction. Until today Wade couldn't ever recall seeing Pearl Lockhart wearing something so short.

She lifted her chin, meeting his gaze straight on.

Despite the rebellious spirit she was currently exhibiting, he couldn't deny that she looked beautiful with her sandy brown hair styled in twists and her clear mocha complexion free of makeup.

What he liked about Pearl was that she always wore a smile, although the one on her face right now was born of pure defiance. She was obviously upset about the conversation they'd had last Sunday regarding her clothes.

The only reason he'd said anything to Pearl in the first place was because he'd overheard some of the teen boys discussing her legs and saying she was the finest woman at Lakeview. Wade hoped to avoid further distractions but he certainly hadn't meant to offend Pearl, the youth-choir director.

"Pastor Kendrick," she began, "I don't think

you should worry about what I'm wearing. God doesn't look at the clothes a person wears. He looks at the heart."

"Miss Lockhart, the Bible speaks about modest clothing," Wade stated calmly. "Scripture tells us that a woman who dresses immodestly causes men to think unholy thoughts. It draws their attention to the outward body, rather than to the inner heart. Just read the third chapter of First Peter."

Wade was not about to be drawn into another debate with her and prayed his response had put an end to the discussion. Pushing away from his desk, he stood up, saying, "It's almost time for service to start. We can continue this conversation after church if you'd like."

Pearl opened her mouth, then shut it.

A muscle flicked angrily at her jaw. Pearl glared at him before storming out of the office and disappearing down the hallway.

Wade released a long sigh. This was not the way he'd planned to start off the morning service. But he would speak with Pearl Lockhart when church ended and clear the air. Apologize if necessary. She and her family had been members of Lakeview Baptist a long time and Wade didn't want a rift to develop between them. He could do without having drama in the church.

When he walked into the sanctuary, Wade found that instead of sitting in her usual seat a few rows back Pearl had made herself comfortable in the front pew, her eyes full of triumph.

She was clearly not going to let this matter drop.

His eyes traveled to her shapely legs, the sight of them stirring something in him. Wade couldn't deny the teenage boys were right. Pearl Lockhart's legs were exquisite.

Stop looking at her legs, he told himself.

Determined in his heart to keep his head and mind on the Lord, Wade signaled for one of the ushers to approach. "Could you please get Miss Lockhart a sheet or blanket, please?"

He stepped up into the pulpit and took his seat between his youth pastor and the assistant pastor. Wade couldn't see her face from where he was sitting, but he could only imagine she was shooting fiery darts through the podium at him with her eyes.

He would have to risk her fury for now because Wade didn't need any distractions, either. It wasn't always easy with church mamas trying to push their daughters in his face and overly aggressive women practically throwing themselves at him.

Wade's mind traveled back to Pearl. He could only assume that she was behaving this way to get his attention. She was a beautiful girl but he didn't go for the boisterous, party-girl type.

Instead, he preferred a woman more like him, conservative, with traditional beliefs. Even with her great body and gorgeous legs, Pearl was definitely not wife material as far as he was concerned.

A tremor of disappointment slid down his spine.

Pearl clamped her jaw tight and stared straight ahead, the blanket folded up beside her on the pew. *How dare Wade Kendrick try to humiliate me like this? The man belongs in the 1800s.*

She found it hard to believe that a man who looked like Wade could be so backward in his beliefs. He stood about six or seven inches taller than her five-foot-four-inch frame, and was lean, muscular and extremely handsome.

Pearl had always found men with bald heads and deep, penetrating eyes incredibly sexy. But

Wade Kendrick was stuffy and took himself way too seriously all the time. She pitied the woman who would eventually marry him.

He couldn't handle a woman like me, that's for sure.

Half of the single women attending Lakeview Baptist were already chasing Wade, but it didn't matter to Pearl. She wanted nothing to do with him.

Even though her anger at him still lay at the surface, Pearl found Wade's sermon on Hosea and Gomer enlightening. He might not have much personality but he was a gifted pastor.

"Why do you look like you're ready to kill somebody?" her cousin Paige Richards asked shortly after service ended. "And why did you sit way up here?"

Before she could respond, her sister Opal walked up, asking, "What's with the leather miniskirt?"

Pearl hugged her in greeting before saying, "Excuse me, Opal. We can talk in a few minutes. Right now I really need to have a word with our pastor."

"Pearl—"

"I won't be long. I promise."

Opal grabbed her by the arm. "That's not what I'm worried about. Pearl, are you still upset over what he said to you? I told you that he didn't mean any harm. I'm sure of it."

Pearl turned around, facing her sister. "He didn't say anything to you. Your dresses are the same length as mine. Ever since the family reunion, he's had it in for me."

"There has to be something more to it."

"Opal, that's exactly what I intend to find out. Don't worry. I just plan to have a quick word with him." She wasn't going to let Wade quote scripture to her and just walk away.

"I don't think it's a good idea, Pearl. The last time…"

She didn't wait around for Opal to finish her sentence. Pearl was on a mission.

She walked with purpose into Wade Kendrick's office. "Pastor, we need to finish our discussion."

He looked up. "Miss Lockhart."

Closing the door halfway, she said, "I need you to explain something to me. Why are you picking on me? Is this about our discussion of women's roles?"

"I'm not picking on you. I never meant to offend you. If I have, I'm sorry."

Did he really think an apology would make things right?

"I appreciate your apology, Pastor," Pearl managed to reply through stiff lips. "However, I still want to know why you singled me out."

"I didn't." Wade paused a moment before continuing. "Please have a seat."

She sat down in one of the chairs facing him.

"The reason I suggested that you lower your hemline is because you're quite a distraction to some of the teen boys here at church."

Pearl was caught off guard by his words. "Excuse me?"

"I overheard some of the boys discussing you. Your legs…"

"Oh." She snapped her mouth shut. Pearl glanced down at the skirt she had on and tried pulling it closer to her knees. She suddenly felt like a fool. "I had no idea, Pastor. I thought you were just being your old stuffy self." She hadn't really meant to say that last part out loud.

Her words seemed to amuse him. "You really consider me stuffy?"

"Yeah, I do."

"I'm not stuffy, Sister Pearl. I just believe that if the church went back to the old way of doing things, we wouldn't have some of the problems we're facing today."

"Such as women not being allowed to wear pants in church? Our last pastor didn't have a problem with women wearing pants to service, but it was one of the first changes you made after taking leadership."

He boldly met her gaze. "Yes. I feel that skimpy dresses or pants show a lack of respect and reverence for the house of God. The Bible clearly states in Deuteronomy that it is a sin for women to wear men's apparel."

"I believe that scripture was referring more to cross-dressers," Pearl countered. "Pastor, have you ever considered that maybe women *should* wear pants to church, so maybe then the boys won't be distracted, as you put it. And you wouldn't need to have ushers bring out the blankets."

He broke into a rare smile.

"Pastor, I'm sorry for my childish behavior this morning. You and I definitely don't see things in the same light, but I'm really not a troublemaker or a hoochie."

"I never thought you were."

Pearl wasn't so sure she believed him but she chose to keep her thoughts at bay.

"I'll give it some thought but I have to be

honest," Wade stated, "I don't think my views will change. It is my goal to make sure that my leadership over this church is biblically sound. I'm going to let the Lord lead me."

"Understood." Pearl got up and walked to the door. "Enjoy the rest of your day, Pastor."

"You, too, Sister Pearl."

As their eyes met, she felt a new and unexpected warmth run through her. Her heart pounding, Pearl walked outside, where she found Opal and Paige waiting by her SUV.

"Pearl, what did you do?"

She eyed her sister. "Opal, I didn't *do* anything. Pastor and I had a talk. A good talk. That's all."

"You mean, you two actually agreed on something?" Opal sounded surprised.

"Naaah, I wouldn't say that. But I think we reached a compromise." Pearl glanced around the parking lot. "Where's Ruby and Amber? Did they leave already?"

"They didn't want to wait around for you to have all of us kicked out of church." When Pearl shot her a look, she added, "I'm only kidding." Laughing, Opal reached over, giving Pearl a hug, then Paige. "I'll see y'all later. I'm meeting D'marcus for brunch."

Opal practically glowed every time she mentioned her boyfriend's name. D'marcus Armstrong was a good man and Pearl considered him fortunate to have her sister in his life.

Pearl drove out of the parking lot and headed for the freeway, driving toward Grosse Pointe, a suburb of Detroit.

Ten minutes later, she drove down Lake Shore Drive and pulled into the garage. Paige parked her BMW Z4 roadster in the space beside her.

The two women walked into the luxury apartment building together.

"Are we still going to the movies later?" Paige asked as they rode the elevator up to the second floor.

Pearl nodded. "Yeah. I just need to take a nap first."

"I could use one myself. Lyman and I didn't get home until two-thirty this morning."

"I was surprised to see you at church. I figured you'd just spend all weekend at his house. Isn't he leaving town this week?"

"Yeah. They're playing Milwaukee on Wednesday."

"I know what we're doing Wednesday night," Pearl said with a grin. Her cousin dated Detroit

Chargers forward Lyman Epse and whenever the team played away from home, Paige and Pearl ordered pizza and watched the game on television. They were both basketball fanatics.

Inside the apartment, Pearl headed straight for the couch. She needed to get out of her boots, which had been clearly designed for fashion, not for comfort.

Her cousin sat down on the chair facing Pearl. "C'mon, what did you really say to Pastor?"

Pulling off the black leather boots with four-inch heels, Pearl related the conversation.

Paige merely stared, tongue-tied. "He really told you that you were distracting the boys?" she asked after a moment.

"Yeah. I don't think he was comfortable with telling me though. I feel like such an idiot now after the way I behaved. I thought he was giving me a hard time because of what happened at the reunion."

"You know what I think? I think Pastor finds you a distraction for himself."

Pearl dismissed her cousin's comment with the wave of her hand.

"I'm serious. I bet he's not telling any of the other women at church to wear longer dresses."

At Pearl's protest, her cousin continued. "Don't you think he's handsome?"

"Yeah, he's nice-looking," she admitted. "But Pastor Kendrick is much too old-fashioned for me."

"If he's interested in you, you better go for it. Honey, if some of the women at church have their way, he won't be single for long. Did you see how Clara was all up in his face a couple of weeks ago? I'm surprised she wasn't at church this morning."

"She's definitely not the woman for him."

Paige broke into a grin. "So who is the woman for him?"

Shrugging, Pearl responded, "I don't know. Sister Barbara is always up in his face—"

Paige laughed. "You wrong, Pearl. She's his secretary."

"She's always trying to get him to have dinner at her house. You should see her. It's shameful."

"Jealous?"

"Me? No way."

Paige rose to her feet. "I'm going to go straighten out my room and get my clothes ready for tomorrow, so I won't have to worry about it when we come home from the movies."

Pearl lay down on the couch. "Wake me when

you're ready to go." She'd worked three double shifts at the restaurant in the past five days and she was dead tired.

She had just closed her eyes when the phone rang. She heard Paige answer on the third ring, then call out for her to pick up.

Pearl grabbed the extension closest to her—it was her manager. She eased up into a sitting position. "It's no problem. I'm glad you called me. I can use the extra money. I'll be there as soon as I can."

When Paige walked back into the living room, Pearl announced, "I'll have to take a rain check on the movies. I need to go in to work."

"Pearl, you need to take some time off."

"I need the money. You know I spent most of my savings on those demo tapes."

"Your sisters and I offered to help you, but you refused."

"Paige, I need to do this for myself. Besides, I'd feel bad if nothing ever comes out of this and I'd taken money from y'all."

"Can you do me a favor and bring me home an order of linguine à la pescatore?"

Pearl nodded. "In fact, I'll pick up a couple of orders. But I'm not getting off until nine."

"That's fine. I'll just eat a late lunch."

Foregoing her nap Pearl made her way to her bathroom. The apartment she and Paige shared came with dual master bedrooms, each with its own glamour bath. She washed her face and freshened up, the hot water being exactly what she needed to bring her tired senses back to life.

Pearl dressed in a pair of black tuxedo pants, a crisp white shirt and a black bow tie. She walked out of her bedroom just as her cousin was about to knock on the door.

"Here's the money for my food," Paige stated, holding out a twenty.

"I'll call you if I get off early."

"Thanks."

Pearl grabbed a short, red leather coat out of the hall closet and headed to the front door. "See you later."

Thirty-five minutes later, Pearl parked on the employee side of the restored Victorian house that had been converted into an upscale Italian restaurant located in the heart of downtown. Milton's Ristorante was considered one of the finest places to dine in Detroit.

Pearl had been working there for almost four years. She enjoyed working on the waitstaff be-

cause the job allowed her the flexibility she
needed for her music and the tips were good.

Still, she dreamed of the day she'd be able to
focus full-time on her music. Pearl knew deep in
her heart that she was destined to be a singer.

Her time would come.

Soon.

Hopefully.

Chapter 2

Wade didn't feel like cooking. In fact, he had grown tired of the variations of Hamburger Helper. He'd eaten enough of it to last him a lifetime.

He reconsidered the invitations issued by a couple of ladies in church. Both Barbara Delany, the church secretary, and Carole Davis came up to him after morning service to invite him over for dinner.

Wade knew without a doubt that the invite from Carole came with strings attached. Shortly after his arrival at Lakeview, Sister Carole became adamant in her attempts to get him to date her daughter, Elizabeth. Wade had taken her to dinner a couple of times.

Liz was nice enough but she was very needy and had a lot of issues. Wade was barely dealing with his own demons, had been for the past ten years. He couldn't take on any additional baggage in his personal life.

He made his way over to the refrigerator and looked inside, noting the bag of salad, a few pieces of fruit and some leftover Hamburger Helper. Wade checked the freezer. He had a steak and a couple of pieces of chicken but they were frozen solid. There was no telling how long they'd been in there and would take too long to thaw out.

The last time he tried to defrost a piece of meat in the microwave… Just the memory was enough to convince Wade not to relive that particular experience. Cooking skills were definitely not among his talents.

Maybe I should seriously consider looking for a wife.

A fleeting image of Pearl Lockhart drifted through his mind. Wade shook his head, trying to shut out all awareness of her.

She's definitely not the woman for me.

His stomach growled loudly.

He briefly considered ordering Chinese food but didn't really have a taste for it. Actually, he was in the mood for pasta. He recalled one of the deacons telling him about a pretty good Italian restaurant in the area.

What was it called? Wade searched his memory.

Milton's, that was it.

He strolled into his office and looked it up on the Internet, searching for details and reviews on the restaurant.

Satisfied with what he'd read, he grabbed his coat, wallet and keys and headed to the door.

Inside his black Chrysler 300, Wade keyed the address into his GPS navigational system. He steered the car out of the driveway and onto the street. He was looking forward to enjoying a meal that hadn't been prepared by his hands or come with somebody's daughter as the dessert.

Fifteen minutes later, Wade arrived at the restaurant. The smell of freshly sautéed garlic and herbs tantalized his senses. A smiling hostess greeted him warmly and escorted him to a small table in the main dining room. The mustard-gold walls and deep burgundy drapes provided a richly colored backdrop while soft music floated throughout the restaurant.

Wade perused the menu while he waited for a member of the waitstaff to arrive. Everything he read on the list sounded delicious.

His eyes traveled around the room, taking in the dining guests and enjoying the ambiance. Wade was more of a homebody unless he was attending a dinner meeting or on a date, but he vowed to change that starting tonight. He'd been in Detroit for a few months. It was time to start enjoying the city.

Humming softly to the music, Pearl carried out a tray of drinks for a party of six. Since coming to work, she'd had a steady stream of customers, but she wasn't complaining. She preferred staying busy. It helped to pass the time.

Pearl was on the schedule to work every day this week except Wednesday, and she'd picked up a singing gig for Saturday.

If things continued the way they were, she'd earn close to fifteen hundred dollars this week— money that would go back into her savings.

Last month she'd sang at three weddings, a function for the mayor of Detroit and a couple of private parties. The gigs had paid well enough to cover her bills for November and December.

Out the corner of her eye, Pearl noted the lone newcomer who had just been seated in her station.

She made her way over to his table.

"Good evening," Pearl greeted. Her voice died when she recognized Wade. "Pastor…hello."

"Sister Pearl," he responded. "I didn't know you worked here."

She lifted her chin, meeting his gaze straight on. "What you mean is that you didn't know I was a waitress."

Wade didn't respond.

Pearl thought she detected a flicker in his intense eyes. "It's okay," she plunged on carelessly. "I'm not ashamed of it. It's a job. I make an honest living. But anyway, welcome to Milton's Ristorante. Have you ever eaten here before?"

"No, this is my first time." Leaning back in his seat, Wade said, "I have a taste for seafood so what would you recommend I try?"

"Everything on the menu is delicious, though I have some personal favorites." She described them in detail, and the pastor made a choice.

"I'll go put your order in and I'll be right back with your water."

Wade nodded in response.

Pearl couldn't believe her luck. Why did Wade Kendrick of all people have to come to Milton's today and end up in her station?

He'd better leave me a nice big tip, she thought to herself.

She returned to Wade's table a few minutes later with his water. Pearl sat it down in front of him, saying, "Your food should be up shortly."

Their gazes met and held, making her uneasy.

"Thank you," he murmured after a moment.

Pearl moved without haste but with hurried purpose. She had no idea why Wade affected her the way he did, but instead of dwelling on the thought, she pushed it to the back of her mind as she wrote down more dinner orders.

She smiled at the two men entering her station, acknowledging them. As soon as they took their seats, Pearl went over to introduce herself.

She stole a peek over her shoulder at the table where Wade was sitting.

He was watching her. Pearl thought she detected a flicker in his intense eyes, causing her pulse to skitter alarmingly.

She drew her attention back to her customers and managed to get through the specials and take their drink order without fumbling. Having Wade seated in her station made her nervous.

But why? she wondered.

Pearl had been completely caught unawares seeing him. Wade was just as surprised to see her standing at his table. She looked as stunning in her uniform as she did any other time. All of the Lockhart siblings were beautiful, but Wade thought Pearl the prettiest.

She was also the most outgoing, it seemed. And the most opinionated, for sure.

His eyes traveled to the two men sitting at the table across from his. They shared similar features, so much that they had to be related to each other. Probably brothers, Wade decided.

Pearl paused at his table to refresh his glass of water, her appearance distracting him briefly from his thoughts.

He cast another smile her way. "Thank you."

"Would you like something else to drink with your dinner besides water?" she inquired.

Wade shook his head. "This is fine."

"Your food should be ready."

While Wade waited for Pearl to come back

with his meal, he reflected back over his life. His journey to the pulpit had not been one without heartache. His gaze landed on the two men laughing and talking nearby, his heart breaking all over again.

I miss you so much, Jeff.

Memories of his dead brother rushed to the forefront, bringing tears to Wade's eyes. Ten years had passed since Jeff's death, but to him, it still felt like it had happened yesterday. Wade didn't know if he would ever be able to escape that particular heartache or be free of the guilt.

It's my fault that Jeff is dead.

Wade had joined the Chicago Kings, one of the city's largest and most violent street gangs, when he was fifteen. Two years later, when his younger brother, Jeff, wanted to join, Wade didn't do anything to dissuade him, despite the constant pleas of their mother.

He knew the dangers, but back then, it was nothing more than a way of life to Wade. It took Jeff being killed in a drive-by shooting a year later to change Wade's way of thinking and to change his life.

Wade went through the motions of eating but not really tasting his food. Seeing families together, enjoying each other, was a constant reminder of everything that he'd lost.

Suddenly needing to get out of there, he dropped two twenty-dollar bills on the table and rose to his feet. He spotted Pearl coming his way and met her.

"I'm sorry but I need to leave," he blurted. "I left money on the table. Keep the change." Wade didn't give her a chance to respond. He walked briskly to the door.

Outside, he took a deep breath and climbed into his car.

Wade pushed his thoughts to the back of his mind as he drove down I-75, en route to his house in Auburn Hills.

At home, Wade went straight to the dresser in his bedroom. From the top drawer he pulled a yellow bandana and a necklace made of gold and black beads—the items Jeff was wearing when he was killed. The faded brownish stains on it were his brother's blood. Wade kept the bandana and necklace because it was all he had left of Jeff.

But the items couldn't help him remember the exact details of what happened that day. Wade had tried over the years to piece together everything, but there was a huge gap in his mind from the time they were walking to a nearby store to his holding Jeff's bullet-ridden body.

Holding the bandana to his chest, Wade sat down on the edge of the king-sized bed, lost in the memories of his brother and the precious little time they'd spent together.

The images Wade dreaded most were of Jeff wearing the bandana and the necklace, and the day Wade took him to get a royal crown tattooed on his shoulder. Wade had since gone through the expensive process of having the Kings's symbol removed via laser treatment. Even now, the faint image of a crown still remained as a permanent link to his past.

"I'm so sorry, Jeff," he whispered, his voice breaking.

Wade would never forget the look on his poor mother's face when she was told that her sixteen-year-old son was dead. She was in denial initially until she looked into Wade's eyes. Her expression changed from grief to pure hatred. She charged at him, beating him with her fists and calling him a murderer.

He winced at the memory.

After they'd buried Jeff, his mother had told him at the cemetery that he no longer had a home or a mother. A close family friend who'd been in town for the funeral had invited Wade to live with his family in Indiana—but only if he was ready to leave the gang.

Harold Green and Wade's father had been in the military together. Afterward they'd both decided to go into law enforcement. Wade's father had been killed five years later when he went to check on a domestic dispute. Uncle Harold had stayed in law enforcement until retiring a few years ago. He'd tried to counsel Wade against gangs, but his words had gone unheard.

Until Jeff's death.

When Jeff died, life with the Chicago Kings no longer appealed to Wade. It had cost him all that had ever mattered to him—his family.

Wade had moved in with the Green family and surprised everyone when he not only accepted Christ into his life, but finished high school and announced that he felt led to ministry. When Harold accepted a position with the Detroit police department, Wade opted to stay in Indianapolis to finish school at the Christian Theological Seminary.

He received a master's of divinity degree with the Green family in attendance. Although he didn't really expect his mother to be in the audience, Wade kept hoping she would come to see him graduate. He missed her dearly.

Wade had not spoken to her in ten years—not since the day they buried Jeff. His death was a wound that would continue to fester and never heal.

Even after her last customer left, Pearl was still wondering what made Wade leave the restaurant in such a hurry. He'd seemed really upset about something.

She cleaned up her station, picked up her dinner and Paige's, then left the restaurant.

She drove straight home, listening to Yolanda Adams's new CD.

Her cousin was waiting for her in the living room. "I'm so glad you're home. I'm starved."

She got up and followed Pearl into the kitchen.

Pearl sat the bag of food on the Venetian gold-granite countertop. "Guess who had dinner tonight at Milton's?"

"Who?" Paige retrieved two plates from one of the cherrywood cabinets.

"Pastor Wade Kendrick."

Paige's eyes widened in surprise. "Really? Was he alone?"

"Yeah. Why?" Pearl wanted to know. "Is he seeing someone?"

"Not that I know of. That's why I was asking you if he was alone."

The thought of Wade with another woman bothered Pearl more than it should've. There was no reason for her to be jealous. They couldn't have a decent conversation much less get involved. Besides, she had absolutely no interest in Wade.

At least that's what Pearl kept telling herself.

Chapter 3

When Wednesday rolled around, Pearl was ecstatic. Tonight the Chargers would play their first game of the season. This afternoon she was meeting Paige at Charlie's Coney Dog Empire, one of Pearl's favorite haunts.

After her errands she made her way to Charlie's, conveniently located across from the hospital where Paige worked, so all her cousin had to do was walk across the street for lunch.

"I'll have two with everything and a cherry Coke," Pearl ordered with a smile. "And these," she added, referring to the bag of potato chips she was holding.

She liked sitting at the counter in full view of the grill, where she could watch the cooks. Her standard order was always two Coney dogs with chili, mustard and raw onions, the toppings piled so high that half of it ended up on her plate.

Paige came up from behind Pearl, wearing a pair of royal blue scrubs beneath her coat. "Hey, girl," she greeted. "How long have you been here?"

"Not very long."

When the waitress came over, Paige ordered, then turned to Pearl. "After I eat this, I'm going to have to spend another hour on the treadmill tonight."

Pearl laughed. "It's so worth it. Besides you'll work it off in the E.R. They usually have you running around like crazy."

"How can you eat all those onions like that?" Paige asked when their food arrived. "You're never going to meet a man walking around with onion breath."

Pearl shrugged. "A little onion breath never killed anyone. Besides, I'm not looking for anyone. I'm content being carefree and single. It gives me a chance to focus on my career."

She said a quick prayer of thanks before taking a bite of her Coney dog. "Mmm, this is so good."

Paige nodded in agreement, her mouth full of food.

While Pearl ate her Coney dog, she contemplated her life. It was true, she was very content with her life but still, there was nothing wrong with some male companionship from time to time. And she wanted to get married one day.

A fleeting image of Wade entered Pearl's mind, surprising her. *Why am I thinking about him?*

"You're not saying much," Paige stated. "Something bothering you?"

"I was just thinking about how it wouldn't be so bad to have a man in my life. You know, it's been a while since I've even been on a date."

"A *long* while."

Pearl nearly choked on her pop. "You didn't have to say it like that. You make it sound like it's been years."

"Well, it has been a while."

"Six months, four days and eight hours, but who's counting?" Pearl responded with a chuckle.

Paige drank some of her pop. "So you're saying that you're ready to be involved in a relationship?"

"If the right person comes along." Pearl

picked up her second Coney dog. "I could eat two more of these."

Shaking her head, Paige said, "You're a heart attack waiting to happen. You should balance out all that junk food with some healthy foods."

"I eat healthy most of the time, and you know it. It's just that I have a thing for Coney dogs and pizza."

"And white chocolate, and red-velvet cake and—"

"I have a sweet tooth, I admit it."

They laughed, and finished their lunch.

"What time are you getting off tonight?" Pearl asked.

"Seven-thirty," Paige responded. "I'll pick up the pizza on my way home."

"They're playing Boston at home on Friday, right?"

Paige nodded. "D'marcus gave Opal our tickets already."

"Great! I'm working the lunch shift but I should be home by five." There was nothing she liked more than watching the game in person.

They talked a few minutes more before Paige went back across the street to Harper University Hospital.

Pearl headed home and spent the rest of the afternoon working on her music. She was composing the arrangements for a new song she'd written for the youth choir to sing. When she first took over as choir director, there was only a handful of teens coming to rehearsal. It wasn't until she began incorporating some of her own original compositions to the playlist that other youth joined the choir. They were now thirty-eight strong, with others wanting to join almost weekly.

Pearl enjoyed working with the teens. They seemed to respect her and they listened to her. She even tutored a couple of them in history.

Detroit had its share of gang activity and Pearl knew that there was a lot of pressure for kids to join a gang. She hoped that by keeping them involved in church activities and stepping up as a role model and mentor she could save them from making a choice that would potentially ruin lives.

Although her father died when she was very young, Pearl had a happy and secure childhood. She grew up feeling safe and loved. But kids today were in crisis and Pearl was committed to doing whatever she could to help them make the right choices.

She was still working on the song when Paige walked into the apartment carrying the pizza.

"Hurry up," Pearl said. "I'll out it on pause until you get out."

She set the pizza down on the counter and rushed off to take a shower.

Meanwhile, Pearl gathered paper plates, napkins and glasses, setting them on the coffee table.

She was seated cross-legged on the floor with the remote in her hand by the time Paige came running out of her bedroom.

"Did I miss anything?"

Pearl shook her head. "It's just starting."

On the first play of the game, the Chargers came down court and Lyman Epse hit a three-pointer.

"Did you just see that?" Paige screamed. "My man just scored three points. Yes!"

Pearl stood up and did a minicheer. "Go, Lyman. That's the way you do it."

She bent down to put a slice of pizza on a plate. Grabbing a napkin, she sat back down on the floor. "Now, that's the way you start a game."

She groaned in agony when the ball was stolen by the other team.

"It's okay," Paige told her. "We're gonna get it back."

"Ooh, I can't stand him," Pearl uttered when

the camera panned to Dashuan Kennedy, Lyman's teammate who was currently on suspension. "It's just something about him."

Paige agreed. "Amber thinks he's gorgeous but I don't see it."

"He's not bad-looking. It's his attitude I don't like. He was so arrogant when Lyman introduced us at that party last month."

"He's been hanging with Kelvin Landy a lot lately."

Pearl didn't know much about the physical therapist and trainer who worked with some Detroit athletes. Shrugging in nonchalance, she said, "Kelvin's okay. It's Dashuan who is such a jerk."

For the rest of the half, they yelled and cheered the Chargers each time they scored.

"You having choir rehearsal tomorrow?" Paige inquired during a commercial break.

Pearl nodded. "I hope Pastor won't be around. He makes me uncomfortable."

Paige finished off her second slice of pizza. "Why?"

"I don't know. He just does," Pearl responded. "Have you noticed that the man hardly ever smiles? He's so serious all of the time."

"Maybe he doesn't have much to smile about,"

Paige offered. "You shouldn't let Pastor get to you like that. He'll keep on if he knows that he can get to you."

"He doesn't *get* to me," Pearl said. But there was no time to argue, as the second half started.

The Chargers were ahead, but not by much. Pearl was on pins and needles until the final buzzer.

"Yes!" She rose up and started dancing. "That's the way to start the season off right. Give Lyman my congratulations when you talk to him," Pearl said. "Meanwhile I'll be in the library working on some music. I've been inspired by the victory."

Thursday morning, Wade strolled into his office at the church, crossing the room to his desk. Up since four-thirty, he'd already spent an hour praying and studying his Bible and taking an early-morning stroll.

Barbara Delany, his secretary, entered the office behind him, carrying a stack of documents.

He quickly looked them over. "Thanks, Barbara. How are you this morning?"

"Blessed and highly favored, Pastor. Oh, my niece is moving back to Detroit this weekend. She's a doctor. An *unmarried* doctor. I can't wait for you to meet her. We're all very proud of her."

A muscle quivered at his jaw. "I'm sure you and she will have a great visit."

"She'll be coming to church with me on Sunday. Marnie's not just coming for a visit. She's going to be working at Detroit Memorial. She wanted to come back home. Our family's very close."

After signing the documents, he handed the papers back to her. "I look forward to meeting her," Wade responded blandly.

Barbara whipped a photo out of her pocket. "I just happen to have a picture of her right here."

Wade politely accepted the photo, eying the woman in it. "She looks like you."

Barbara broke into a big grin. "That's what everybody says."

Wade sent up a silent prayer for any type of interruption to jolt Barbara back into secretary mode. Why didn't members of his congregation trust him to pick his own wife?

As if heaven sent, the telephone began to ring.

"I better go get that," Barbara uttered, rushing out of the office.

Wade sent up a quick prayer of thanks.

She put the call through to his office and he answered on the second ring, "Pastor Wade Kendrick."

"Wade, it's Harold. Hadn't talked to you in a couple of days. Wanted to say hello."

He smiled. Harold Green and his family had always been a part of his extended family, but for the past ten years they were his only family.

"I had you on my list to call today," Wade stated. "I wanted to invite you to lunch, if you have some time today."

"Ivy and Cassie are doing some last-minute shopping for the wedding. I have a few hours to kill. Lunch is good."

They arranged a time and a place.

Wade met Harold at the restaurant shortly after twelve.

"Uncle Harold," he greeted, "I'm glad you could meet me."

They followed a hostess to a small table by the window. When they were seated, Harold asked, "How are things going at Lakeview?"

"Well, I'm adjusting," Wade responded. "Some of the mothers in the church are trying to marry me off to their daughters. That's a good sign, I think."

Harold chuckled. "You can't be surprised. You're a minister of a medium-sized church, you have a nice car, you're good-looking. Man, that makes you a good catch."

Wade changed the subject by asking, "So how are the wedding plans going?"

Sighing in resignation, Harold answered, "My wife and my daughter are getting sick of each other. I'm glad the wedding is this Saturday. I don't know how much longer I can referee."

Wade chuckled. "Weddings are supposed to be happy occasions."

"But the planning is a nightmare. Ivy wants to throw rice while Cassie only wants birdseed and her future mother-in-law thinks they should just release a couple of doves. *Doves.* Have you heard of such a thing?"

"I've had some similar requests but as long as it's not done in the church, I don't have a problem with it," Wade stated. "I know Cassie. She's going to have her way in this. She's as stubborn as Aunt Ivy."

Harold agreed. "And it's driving my wife crazy. I keep telling Ivy that this is our daughter's wedding, not hers."

The waitress arrived to take their food and drink orders.

While they waited for the food, Harold announced, "I spoke to your mother last week. She sounded good."

"That's great news," Wade replied. "I'm glad to hear that."

"Have you tried to call her lately?"

A pain squeezed his heart as Wade thought about his estranged mother. "No point in it. She's never going to forgive me for Jeff's death. She hasn't spoken to me since he died and she's not going to talk to me now."

"How do you know unless you try?"

"Uncle Harold, I've tried. You know that. I used to call once a month, then three times a year. She won't talk to me. All she does is slam the phone down as soon as she realizes it's me."

"You should never give up on family, Wade."

"I haven't given up," he stated. "My mother was the one who gave up on me."

"Your mother loves you," Harold said. "One day she'll remember just how much."

Wade didn't want to continue this conversation because it hurt too deeply. He changed the topic to sports, which dominated their thoughts until lunch was over.

Wade returned to his office to find Melinda Newberry, one of the church members, waiting for him. He released a short sigh, then pasted on a smile.

"Sister Melinda, it's nice to see you. What brings you here?"

"I'm attending the Grosse Pointe Heart Foundation gala next weekend and I thought maybe you could escort me. Pastor, it would be the perfect chance for you to meet some very influential people here in Detroit. It would be nice for them to meet you, as well."

Wade tried to think of a way to let her down gently. "Thank you for the invitation, but I'm afraid I won't be able to attend."

She looked offended. "I just thought it would be nice for you to network. Some of Detroit's most prominent ministers will be in attendance. Pastor, you really should be there." She gave him a sexy smile. "Won't you reconsider?"

"I'm afraid I can't," he replied. "Thank you for thinking of me."

Without a response, Melinda strode out of the building in a huff.

"You did the right thing, Pastor," his secretary told him. "She's after fame and fortune. I'm not one to gossip but the truth is the light. Melinda Newberry only wants a man with money."

He laughed. "Then I don't have a thing to worry about."

Wade headed to his office.

Barbara followed him. "Now, my niece… she's a real nice girl. But I have to tell you that she's not looking for a boyfriend. Marnie wants a husband. She's ready to settle down and have a lot of pretty babies."

"I'll keep her in my prayers," Wade stated.

"I appreciate you remembering her in your prayers, Pastor, but I'd like for you to meet her. I'll make sure I introduce you to Marnie. I'm telling you, she's a nice girl. Just needs to be married."

Wade didn't miss the not-so-subtle hint but chose not to comment on it. When the time was right, God would bring into his life the woman he was meant to marry.

Until then, Wade had to run in the other direction whenever Barbara and the other women threw their daughters in his direction.

Pearl was so exhausted, she could barely think straight. Not even a shower woke her up.

Paige was in the living room watching television when she walked out. "Hey, girl," she greeted. "You look like you need to go back to bed."

"Don't tempt me," she moaned. "My manager just called. I'm going in early today, picking up another shift."

"You can't work all those hours at Milton's and then do your singing gigs. Just thinking about it makes me tired, too."

"Hopefully, I won't have to do this much longer. I pray I'll get a record deal from the demo tapes I sent out."

"You will," Paige assured her. "I believe it."

Pearl stretched out on the sofa. "Lord, give me strength."

"Why don't you just stay home today?"

"I need the money, Paige."

"But if you'd let us—"

Pearl cut her off. "I've told you a thousand times that I appreciate you and my sisters for wanting to help, but this is something I need to do for myself."

As if on cue, her sister Ruby called.

Glancing over at the clock, Pearl answered saying, "Why are you calling here so early? It's not even eight-thirty."

She laughed when her oldest sister responded, "I know you aren't still in bed."

"I should still be, though. I stayed up late working on a song."

Ruby was the pragmatist of all the Lockhart sisters. Since their mother's death five years ago, she'd been thrown into the role of the matriarch and constantly harped on the importance of family.

Even now, she was calling just to check on Pearl. If Ruby didn't hear from her siblings every couple of days, she began calling around.

"Did you watch the game last night?" Pearl asked, although she already knew the answer. Ruby wasn't into sports the way she was. Neither was Amber; she just liked going to the games in hopes of meeting someone. Since D'marcus was a co-owner of the Chargers franchise, Opal would go with them from time to time.

"No. I didn't get a chance to see it. I had some work to do."

Before ending the call, Pearl made plans to have lunch with her sister soon. She loved Ruby, but was growing tired of her pushing Pearl to go back to college like Opal and finish up her degree.

It had been her mother's deepest wish that they all get college degrees, but that wasn't where Pearl's heart lay. She wanted to sing.

Singing had always been her dream and Pearl was not about to give up on the true desire of her heart.

Chapter 4

Trinity Church on Mackinac Island provided the perfect setting for a fall wedding. The rows of seating were garnished with riots of red and orange roses arranged with gold ribbons and baby's breath.

Bridesmaids adorned in beige gowns and carrying bouquets of flowers bursting in orange, yellow and gold floated down the aisle escorted by handsome groomsmen dressed in black tuxedos.

The bride made her grand entrance wearing a designer wedding dress in cream and holding an eye-catching bouquet in beauteous, brilliant, warm tones of red and orange.

Pearl glanced down at her own gown, a burnished red. She loved vivid color, avoiding neutral tones like the ones she saw among the guests at the Hamilton-Green wedding when she stood up to sing.

Her eyes lit on one guest in particular. Wade Kendrick. She was entranced by the silent sadness of his face. He'd worn that same look that day at the restaurant.

Once again, she wondered at the cause.

The groom had requested that Pearl perform a special love song, one she'd written just for them. A romantic at heart, Pearl found the task easy.

When she finished singing, the applause was thunderous. Humbled, Pearl smiled, and then took her seat. She was in her element whenever she was singing. She loved being in front of an audience, though initially she had felt a little nervous with Wade sitting in the congregation.

Pearl had no idea why she'd been so nervous. Wade had heard her sing plenty of times at church. But somehow, this time felt different. Maybe it was because she was singing in such a romantic setting.

When the ceremony ended, she found Wade

standing beneath a huge elm tree outside of the church. Guests stood scattered around the picturesque grounds of the Mission Hills Resort while the bridal party returned to the church inside to take wedding pictures.

"Hello, Pastor."

"Sister Pearl, it's nice to see you. That song you sang was beautiful. I don't think I've ever heard it before."

She smiled at the compliment and felt an unwelcome surge of excitement within her. "Thank you. I wrote it. It's my gift to the bride and groom."

What am I doing? Pearl wondered to herself. She glanced up at him to find Wade watching her.

She searched for something to say. "The ceremony was nice, don't you think?"

He agreed. "Are you staying for the reception?"

"Yes. Why?"

"I thought this would be a good time to get to know each other. I want you to see that I'm really not a bad person."

A delicious shudder heated her body. "Pastor, I never thought you were a bad person. Just old-fashioned and judgmental."

He laughed, surprising her. "Are you always this blunt?"

"It's the only way I know how to be. What you see is what you get when it comes to me."

"I'm not so sure I agree with that," he replied cryptically.

Folding her arms across her chest, Pearl uttered, "Excuse me?"

"It's not a bad thing, by any means. I just meant, there's a lot more to you than meets the eye."

She cleared her throat, pretending not to be affected by his words. "Everyone is going into the reception," Pearl stated. "We should find our tables."

She chewed on her bottom lip as Wade escorted her into the Cypress Ballroom where they discovered that they were assigned to the same table. "Looks like we're going to be sitting together," Pearl said. She was filled with a strange inner excitement.

He smiled in response. "This confirms that we should get to know each other."

"If you say so, Pastor."

Wade guided her over to their table and pulled out a chair for her.

"Thank you," Pearl murmured as she sat down, her heart hammering foolishly.

I've got to stop this, she told herself. She watched him as he dropped down into the chair beside her, noting how handsome Wade looked in the black suit he was wearing. It fit him as if it had been designed just for him.

Pearl was totally entranced by his compelling personage. *Too bad he's not my type.*

"I have to admit that I'm very surprised to see you here," she confessed. "Are you a friend of the bride or the groom?"

"The bride," Wade responded. "Cassie Green's family and I go way back. Her father is actually the reason I applied to Lakeview Baptist in the first place. He told me the church needed a pastor."

"I didn't know that." Switching topics, she asked, "Have you ever been here before? To Mackinac Island?"

Shaking his head, Wade responded, "This is my first time."

"So did you enjoy taking the ferry over?" No cars were allowed on the island, so guests were delivered to the church via horse-drawn carriages.

He nodded. "I couldn't imagine an island without cars, but it's nice and scenic over here."

After the bride and groom danced the first time as husband and wife, it was time for the other guests to join them on the dance floor. Pearl and Wade found themselves alone at their table.

"This is probably a silly question," she asked, "but do you dance?"

"I love dancing. I just haven't done it in a long time."

She eyed him in amazement.

"What?"

"I guess I expected you to say that you didn't know how," she confessed, pushing back a strand of hair. "I'm shocked, but then again, I haven't seen you dance. I'm not sure you have any rhythm."

Wade laughed. "Why? Because you think I'm such a stuffed shirt?"

Grinning, Pearl responded, "Something like that."

"Sister Pearl, I've never claimed to be a saint. I'm far from it."

She gave him a sidelong glance. "So do you want to give it a try? Would you like to dance with me?"

"Sure."

Pearl stood up, waiting for Wade to escort her to the dance floor. She walked slowly, her body swaying to the music. "I love this song."

Wade took her to the middle of the dance floor and began moving to the music.

She was impressed. He was a really good dancer.

The song ended and another began while they were still on the dance floor. Wade didn't guide Pearl back to their table until a slow song came on.

"I have to confess I didn't think you had it in you."

Stroking his chin, Wade responded, "Miss Lockhart, believe it or not, I actually know how to have a good time."

"What constitutes a good time to you?" she questioned. "What is it that you do for fun?"

"I read."

"Something other than the Bible?"

Wade chuckled. "I happen to enjoy mystery thrillers and I read a lot of science fiction, too."

The warmth of his smile echoed in his voice. "Interesting. Who's your favorite author?"

"James Patterson. I'm reading his latest novel at the moment. Tell me, what do you do for fun?"

"I love the water so I spend a lot of time at the beach during the summer," she responded. "I'm a history buff so I'm always taking tours and doing research. And, of course, I love music."

"I love history myself. In fact, I've been reading some books on the history of Detroit."

"Have you ever been to the Charles H. Wright Museum of African-American History?"

"I plan on going. I've heard the exhibits are fantastic."

Pearl agreed. "My favorite is the one where you travel through time. You start your journey in prehistoric Africa. Then you watch the evolution of ancient civilizations. I got really emotional crossing the Atlantic Ocean—"

"The middle passage," Wade interjected.

She nodded. "That part of our history is painful but it's also an inspiration to me when I think of our ancestors fighting to end the horrors of bondage and striving to build a legacy of freedom for future generations. You definitely have to see it, Pastor."

"I'd like to experience that journey." Wade held her gaze. "Is there anything else I should see?"

"I'm sure you've been to the Motown Museum, right?" Pearl glanced over at his well-defined profile. Wade was a good-looking man, she couldn't deny that.

"I have," he confirmed. "I've also been to the original Dunbar Memorial Hospital."

"When the hospitals denied care to African-Americans, several doctors formed the Allied Medical Society, who then acquired the Charles W. Warren House and converted it into a hospital in 1917. Dunbar Hospital didn't just provide care, they also sponsored nurses' training classes and internships for graduate students. Did you know that?"

"You really are into your history, aren't you?"

She broke into a grin. "I told you. I love history."

Their conversation drew to a halt when Harold and Ivy Green walked over to where they were dancing. Wade hugged Ivy and shook hands with Harold.

He then introduced Pearl.

Aunt Ivy complimented her. "You were absolutely wonderful. Your singing moved me to tears."

"Thank you," Pearl murmured in response. "The ceremony was very inspiring. Your daughter is a beautiful bride." As she spoke to Ivy, she was ever conscious of Wade beside her, his good looks, his virile appeal. And it bothered Pearl. An attraction to Wade would be perilous.

"Wade," Uncle Harold began, "I want to introduce you to a good friend of mine who's here. Bob Whitfield used to work with me and your father. He left six months before your dad passed."

Turning to Pearl, Wade said, "I'll be right back."

She was thankful to have some time alone to gather herself.

Girl, you need to get a hold of yourself, she silently chided. *Stop acting like you're in heat.*

Wade returned to the table ten minutes later. "I'm sorry about that. I don't come across many people who knew my father much."

"I understand totally."

The band began playing a familiar song, which Pearl sang along to. Her eyes traveled over to Wade. Giving him a sheepish grin, she said, "I love that one, too."

Wade gave her a smile that sent her pulse racing.

It was time then for the bride to throw the bouquet.

"Shouldn't you be up there with the rest of the single women?"

Pearl wrinkled her nose and shook her head. "I'm not about to make a fool of myself over some flowers, no matter how beautiful they are."

"You're not superstitious, are you?"

"Naaah." Pearl pushed away from the table. "What I need is to get some air. It's stuffy in here." As an afterthought, she added, "Care to join me?"

Wade rose to his feet. "Sure."

He followed her as she navigated through the

sea of people in the ballroom. She was just a few yards from the door when a flash of vivid color floated across the room.

Pearl gasped in surprise as the bouquet fell into her hands. Wade threw back his head, cracking up with laughter.

Before she could utter a word, cameras were flashing all around her. She glanced over at Wade, who was still laughing. "What's so funny?"

"I wish you could see the expression on your face."

Grinning, Pearl responded, "With all these cameras I'm sure I will." Loving the attention, she posed for a series of pictures before escaping through the nearest door with Wade.

She was still clutching the bridal bouquet when she stepped outside in her coat. "It's cold but it feels better out here than inside." Truth be told, she didn't know whether she was having hot flashes or if just being around Wade was making her overheated.

"It's nice out here."

She gave Wade a sidelong glance. "I heard Mr. Green say that your father passed away. How long ago did it happen?"

"When I was fourteen. My dad was a policeman. He was killed on the job."

"We have something in common, then. My father died when I was eight years old. He was a policeman, too, and killed in the line of duty." She glanced up at him. "Were you and your father close?"

"He was my best friend. What about you?"

"I loved my daddy like crazy. I keep a picture of him by my bed. Losing him was hard but when my mother died five years ago, I thought I'd lose my mind."

"How did she die?"

"She had pancreatic cancer. Mama died three months after the diagnosis. We didn't even have a chance to get used to the fact that she had cancer." After a brief pause, Pearl said, "Okay, enough of this kind of talk. We're at a wedding reception."

"The celebration is winding down." Wade checked his watch. "I guess I'll head back to the ferry in a few minutes."

"Hey, do you want to go on a tour?" Pearl blurted, surprising herself. "If you'd like, I can rent a carriage and drive you around."

His eyebrows rose in astonishment. "You can handle a horse and buggy?"

"Yeah. I love horses and I've been riding since I was ten."

"But have you ever driven a carriage?"

"Not really," Pearl confessed with a grin. "But it can't be that hard."

"Why don't we just hire a driver to take us around?" Wade suggested.

Folding her arms across her chest, Pearl inquired, "You don't trust my skills, Pastor?"

"It's not that. I just thought we could enjoy the tour together."

Pearl broke into a short laugh. "Careful, Pastor. You're dangerously close to fibbing."

Wade chuckled. "I think we've been around each other long enough for you to call me by my given name."

"Only if you call me by mine."

"Agreed."

Pearl ventured off to make the arrangements for their tour of the island. She returned a few minutes later saying, "It's all set. We're taking a carriage ride."

They made small talk as they waited for the horse and buggy to arrive.

Wade assisted Pearl into the carriage. He followed, sitting beside her.

She reached for the blanket and covered up. "It's beautiful out here but cold. You're going to have to come back in the summer for one of the lighthouse cruises."

"I'll keep that in mind."

As the carriage took them around the island, Pearl pointed out the sights, adding interesting details and amusing anecdotes.

When the carriage came to a stop, Wade turned to her. "I'm enjoying the ride and the company. Thank you for doing this, Pearl."

Their eyes locked, sending her heart hammering against her ribs. She struggled to rein in her emotions.

A man sits beside me and I'm about to fall apart. I know it's been six months since my last date but this is crazy.

"Pearl," Wade prompted.

"Huh?" She came out of her reverie.

"I think you were going to tell me something about the lighthouse. You told the driver to stop here."

"Oh, yeah," she mumbled, her heart hammering foolishly. "The lighthouse."

"Thanks for the tour," Wade said when they were seated on the ferry back to the mainland. "You know a lot about this place."

"You're quite welcome, Wade." She flashed him another of those million-dollar smiles that had mesmerized him on the carriage ride. His gaze slid downward, moving over her body slowly, enjoying the view. He gave himself a mental shake.

"I'm sure you're as knowledgeable about Chicago," Pearl said.

Wade nodded. "I am. Born and raised there until I was eighteen."

Where did you move to after that?"

"Gary, Indiana."

"So you didn't move too far from Chicago?"

"Not at all."

"Do you like living in Detroit?"

"I do," he answered, then posed a question of his own. "So how did you end up singing at Cassie's wedding?"

"I know Roger Hamilton's family. They're friends with Luther Biggens, who's like a brother to me. I think you met him at the family reunion. But I actually get invited to sing at a lot of weddings and other events."

"I'm not surprised. You have a lovely voice." He smiled at her. "I remember meeting Luther. He's the one who owns the car dealerships."

Pearl nodded. "Did you enjoy yourself at the family reunion?"

"I had a real good time."

"Until our debate, huh?"

He laughed.

"You really don't have a problem sharing your opinions, do you?"

"Why should I? Besides, the way I see it, you and I have that in common. I couldn't believe how you called me out on the length of my skirt like that." She laughed. "I wanted to strangle you, Wade."

"I see you have a violent streak, as well," he responded. "We're going to have to take that to the altar." Wade couldn't resist teasing her.

Pearl laughed. "I can't believe you said that to me. Especially sitting right beside me. You're a brave man."

He liked the sound of his name on her lips. "I've got the Lord on my side. Seriously though, I just didn't want you distracting our boys, but some things are just beyond my control."

The amused look suddenly left her eyes. "Explain yourself."

"Pearl, you're a very beautiful young woman. You attract a lot of attention."

"I'm not *trying* to do that."

Wade raised his brows inquiringly. "You love attention. There's nothing wrong with that."

"Okay. I'll admit that I do enjoy it. But to be a singer you have to love a fair amount of attention."

"It's not a criticism, by any means."

"You draw a certain amount of attention yourself, you know?"

"That's because I'm in the pulpit. I—"

Pearl cut him off. "Hardly. Wade, you're a handsome man. That's a draw—even for a man in ministry."

"And all this time I was thinking it was my soul-stirring sermons that had the pews filled every Sunday."

"You can preach, but most of the honeys crowding the first three rows are there to check you out. Trust me."

He laughed.

"I don't mean any disrespect, but I'm telling the truth. Hey, whatever it takes to get 'em in the church—that's what I say. Work it, Pastor."

"What am I going to do with you?" Wade had never seen this side of Pearl, but he liked it. She was a chameleon, which was probably why the youth at church loved her. She was skilled in her ability to relate to both the adults and the teens.

He believed Pearl definitely had a wild side to her, but seemed to keep her life in balance. Wade admired that about her.

"We should head toward the exit," she said. "The ferry's about to dock."

He nodded in agreement. Deep down, Wade felt a thread of disappointment that their time together was coming to an end.

Pearl's mind was still on Wade Kendrick when she arrived home. A quiver surged through her body as she recalled how much she had enjoyed his company. The fact that they hadn't disagreed once only added to her pleasure. Maybe she'd made the wrong assumption about him.

"We had a nice time," Pearl whispered to her empty bedroom. "The pastor and I. He's not as bad as I thought."

Paige wasn't home, so she changed into something more casual and strolled into the library, where her keyboard was set up in one corner of the room. Pearl sat down and began playing.

She gave up after only an hour because her

mind just wasn't on her music. She was still thinking about Wade and their carriage ride after the reception. Pearl hoped that she hadn't been too
forward with him.

But it's true. Wade is fine.

Restless, with Wade still dominating her
thoughts, Pearl walked over to the treadmill sitting
by the window in her bedroom, trying to ignore
the strange aching in her limbs. She turned it on
and began a steady, slow pace.

*Maybe this will work this man out of my sys-
tem,* Pearl thought to herself.

"Wade, you're driving me crazy," she whispered. "I need you to stop it. Just stop it."

She didn't stop jogging until she reached her
personal goal of three miles. Pearl could barely
walk but she managed to drag herself to the
shower.

Even the exercise didn't tire her mind and her
racy thoughts of Wade. It was after midnight but
she still struggled with falling asleep.

Pearl began singing the lullaby her mother used
to sing. Her eyes grew wet.

"Mama, I miss you so much. Why did you have
to leave when I need you so much?"

Chapter 5

Pearl was looking forward to service this morning, although she kept telling herself that it had nothing to do with Wade.

She'd enjoyed showing him around Mackinac Island but Pearl refused to make more out of it. It was nothing more than a simple carriage tour. She would've done that for anybody, she rationalized.

When Paige was ready, they left for church. Pearl had to be there early because the youth choir was singing this morning.

"You never did tell me how the wedding was,"

Paige said. "I bet it was beautiful. The Hamiltons know how to make any celebration the event of the year. I don't know anything about the bride's family."

"They're the reason Wade…uh, Pastor Kendrick is here in Detroit. They're close friends of his family."

"I guess he was at the wedding, then?"

Pearl nodded as they walked down to the parking garage. "Yeah. I gave him a tour of Mackinac Island."

"Wade, huh?" Paige murmured. "So you two are on a first-name basis? And you two took a horse-and-buggy ride around the island? How very romantic."

Ignoring Paige, she unlocked the doors to her SUV. "Get in the car."

"You and Pastor must've had *some* conversation yesterday at the wedding."

Her accusing tone grated Pearl's nerves. "Drop it already. There is nothing going on between us."

"Then why are you acting so defensive?"

"I'm not," Pearl replied a little too quickly. "I was only trying to be sociable. The man is the pastor of the church I attend."

"Uh-huh. If you say so."

The short drive to Lakeview Baptist seemed longer than usual.

"I've got to go check on my chair," Pearl announced as she parked the car. "I'll see you in the church."

The first person Pearl ran into was Wade when she entered the doors leading to the administration building. Choir members gathered in one of the classrooms to wait for their processional. She pasted on a smile and prayed that Paige had decided to stay inside the sanctuary.

"Good morning, Pearl," Wade greeted warmly.

"'Morning," she responded.

He glanced around before saying, "I had fun yesterday. Thank you for the tour."

"You don't have to keep thanking me. I didn't mind at all."

Pearl changed the subject when a couple of church members walked by. "I'm going to need to pick up some new music for the choir."

"Just leave the information on my desk, if you will. I'll take a look at everything and get back to you."

"The proposal's ready. I'll drop it off in your office right now." Pearl cleared her throat softly. "See you around, Pastor."

She moved around him, walking with purpose. Pearl nodded at a few people on her way to the classroom where the choir members had gathered.

Pearl heard someone call out her name and stopped walking. She turned around to find Justine Raymond coming toward her, swinging her wide hips from left to right.

"I need to talk to you for a minute," the woman called.

Clenching her mouth tight, Pearl waited for Justine to reach her. No matter how hard she tried to get along with Justine, there was always drama in one form or another.

"I saw you talking to Pastor Kendrick." Lowering her voice to a whisper, she asked, "He is so fine, don't you think?"

"Justine—"

"Girl, you know he is, just admit it." Her smile disappeared. "You trying to get with him?"

"No. Not at all."

"I'm so glad to hear that. Because I'm definitely trying to make him mine." Justine tried unsuccessfully to pull down the tight-fitting sweater dress she was wearing. "Give me about six months and, girl, you gonna be singing at our wedding."

Pearl laughed to cover her annoyance. "Good luck with that, Justine."

"You think I'm playing, but I'm dead serious. That man is mine."

"Justine, I don't want to be rude but I have to check on my choir. I need to get them lined up and ready to march in."

"I just wanted to let you know what's up, so you wouldn't be wasting your time." Justine sashayed down the hall, her long burnished red mane bobbing as she walked.

Pearl stared after her, shaking her head in disbelief. *How dare she confront me like this?* She knew Justine was just being her usual self, running her mouth and thinking every man in Lakeview Baptist was interested in her.

The real question was why she was so bothered by it?

Wade had just walked into his office when Barbara suddenly appeared in the doorway with her niece; a tall, curvaceous young woman with shiny black curls hanging down her back.

"This is Marnie. She's my sister's youngest child. Dr. Marnie Anderson."

"It's nice to meet you, Dr. Anderson."

"Just call me Marnie, Pastor." Her eyes traveled down the length of his body. "Auntie has told me so many wonderful things about you. I enjoyed your sermon this morning."

"Thank you." He felt her eyes rake over him, and looked for an escape.

Relief washed over him when he spotted Pearl walking by his office. Rushing to the doorway, he impulsively called out to her, "Sister Pearl."

To Barbara and Marnie, he uttered, "Excuse me, please," as he left the office.

Pearl waited for him to catch up.

"What's up?"

"I…" Wade cleared his throat. "I'm sorry. I just needed to—"

"Escape?" Pearl interjected with a chuckle. "Pastor, are you using me to get away from the doctor and her matchmaking aunt?"

"Guilty. I hope I haven't offended you."

She laughed. "Actually, I think it's funny. Don't worry, I'll walk you out to your car but, you know, you owe me."

"What do you have in mind?"

She shrugged in response. "Let me give it some thought."

Wade stole a peek over his shoulder. Barbara and her niece were standing outside his office, watching his verbal exchange with Pearl.

"Doesn't look like they're going anywhere, Pastor. My guess is that you should just go back there and turn her down gently."

Pearl didn't bother to hide the amusement in her voice. She was having fun at his expense. "You should see the look on your face."

"You're really enjoying this, aren't you?"

"Seeing you look uncomfortable? Yeah, I am. Enjoy the rest of your day, Pastor."

"Pastor," Barbara said loudly, interrupting their conversation.

Pearl peeked around him. "Oh, don't worry about owing me that favor now. I don't think they're going to let you get away so easily."

He could hear her chuckling as she walked away.

Sighing in resignation, Wade walked back over to where Barbara and Marnie stood.

"Pastor, I was just telling Auntie that you should join us this afternoon for Sunday dinner. I hate to brag but I can throw down in the kitchen."

Wade searched for an excuse to turn down the invitation. "I don't want to inconvenience you and Barbara. Thank you for the invite. Another time perhaps."

Marnie looked like she wanted to try to change his mind but she clamped her mouth shut.

Barbara spoke up. "My niece is telling the truth, Pastor. She can cook up a storm."

"We'll give Pastor advance notice the next time, Auntie. This will give me time to really impress him with my skills." She winked at Wade. "Why don't we plan on one night during the week?"

He couldn't believe Marnie flirted so brazenly in front of her aunt. To him, it showed a lack of respect. He cleared his throat noisily before saying, "I'll check my calendar and get back to you."

The next morning, Wade was at the church earlier than usual.

He eyed the date on the calendar with a heavy heart.

November twelfth.

Today was his father's birthday. Wade opened his wallet, revealing a family photograph. He recalled how happy they were the day that picture was taken.

His father died a month later. His death left a

void in Wade's life, in all of their lives, really. His mother suddenly found herself a widow and the head of their household. Jeff looked to him as a father figure and Wade…he sought to reclaim all that he'd lost—a sense of family. A sense of belonging.

The Chicago Kings provided that for him. Before his death, Wade's father worked diligently to keep the city safe from gang violence. If he knew that his son had joined a gang—something he was so against—he would be so disappointed in him.

"Maybe if you were still here, Jeff would still be alive," he said to his father.

Wade didn't doubt that he would have ended up preaching, he'd had that calling on his life since he was a child. His paternal grandfather was a minister and Wade used to spend a lot of time with him at his church. He'd always felt at home in the pulpit.

A second photo in the wallet was one of his grandparents. They died in a car accident the year before his father was killed. He had just begun to get over their deaths when he lost his dad.

Wade picked up the cupcake he purchased earlier. "Happy birthday, Dad," he whispered before taking a bite.

He could hear the telephone ringing and his secretary's voice when she answered. A few seconds later, she put the call through.

"Hello."

"Wade, this is Uncle Harold. How are you?"

"I'm doing okay," he responded. "I guess you know what day it is."

"Yeah. It's your father's birthday today."

"He was a great man. I…" Wade's voice died. There were no words to describe his feelings at the moment. He idolized his father and knowing that he'd let him down by getting Jeff killed only made Wade feel worse.

"I had a feeling I'd find you here."

Startled, Pearl glanced over her shoulder. "Luther, I didn't hear you walk up. You nearly scared me to death."

"Sorry. I didn't mean to scare you."

She tried to shake off the momentary feeling of fear she'd experienced. "How on earth did you know I'd be here? I didn't tell anyone I was coming to the cemetery."

Luther Biggens walked slowly up the hill to where Pearl sat cross-legged on the grass. He walked with a slight limp, the result of his stepping on a land mine during his Navy SEAL days. The leg he lost had been replaced by a prosthetic limb. His father and hers had been close friends since childhood. Luther was the big brother she'd never had and she adored him.

"I was actually driving by and I saw your car."

Pearl reached forward, tracing the letters on her father's headstone. "I know this may sound strange to you but when I come out here, I feel close to my parents. I miss them so much."

Luther nodded in understanding. "I miss them, too."

"I was just telling them about the demo."

"Have you heard back from any of the record companies?"

Shaking her head, Pearl answered, "Not yet. Hopefully, I'll hear something soon."

He smiled. "You will. Pearl, you're an incredible singer and songwriter."

"Let's hope that the record companies feel the same way. I'm getting tired of working all those doubles at Milton's. Luther, all I want to do is sing. It's all I've ever wanted and dreamed about. Some days I just know I'm going to make it but then on other days...I'm not that confident."

"I have all the confidence in the world because you want it so badly. It's all you've ever talked about."

"Maybe I'm asking too much. Maybe this isn't going to happen for me. I—"

Luther interrupted her by saying, "Don't do that. You can't start thinking negatively."

"You're right." Pearl glanced up at Luther. "Would you like to have lunch with me? I'm starving and if I don't eat something soon, I'm going to pass out."

"We can't have that," he responded with a smile. "There's nothing I'd like better than to have lunch with you."

"Unless it's with Ruby," Pearl murmured.

"What are you talking about?"

Laughing, Pearl murmured, "Nothing, Luther. Nothing at all." She allowed Luther to assist her to her feet.

"Instead of matchmaking, why don't you find a man for yourself?"

"Ouch."

He chuckled.

They walked side by side down the grassy hillside toward their cars. "I can't believe you just said that to me, Luther."

He cast a look in her direction. "Why? Don't

you ever think about settling down? I heard you caught the bouquet at Roger's wedding."

"It was practically handed to me. Cassie threw it straight at me because I was with Wade. I think she was aiming for him. But, yeah. I'd like to settle down one day. I just need to find Mr. Right."

"What about your pastor?"

"Wade?" Unlocking her car, Pearl asked, "What about him?"

"I hear he's a single man. He seems nice enough."

Pearl glanced back at Luther. "And?"

"You don't have any interest in him?"

"Why would you ask me something like that?" Pearl questioned. Frowning, she asked. "Have you been talking to my sisters?"

Luther headed to his car but not before querying, "Where are we eating?"

"Just follow me."

They drove to a nearby restaurant. After being seated and placing their orders, Pearl and Luther settled down to catch up. The subject of education came up.

"I really wish Ruby would let this go," Pearl said.

"Your mother made her promise to make sure

that you and your sisters went to college and finished your education. Ruby's just trying to keep her word."

"I understand all that, Luther. But I need Ruby to understand that I'm a singer. I want to sing."

"She knows," Luther stated. "Ruby wants you to achieve your dreams. She's very proud of you."

"I know that. My sister wants me to do both—sing and get my degree. It's just that I'm not interested in going back to school. Opal's in college and she's graduating soon. That should be enough for now."

"What's Amber been up to?"

"Being Amber," responded Pearl. "You know my sister. She's the one Ruby should be worried about." She sliced off a piece of grilled chicken and stuck it into her mouth. "What have you been up to, Luther? I don't think I've seen you since the family reunion."

"We just opened a new dealership in Auburn Hills."

"Congratulations," Pearl murmured. "So what is it this time? Mercedes, Honda or BMW?"

"Honda," Luther responded.

"I have some friends over in Auburn Hills. I'll let them know so they can check out the dealership."

"Please do. I want to sell as many cars as I

can." Luther wiped his mouth with the corner of his napkin. "Did you save room for dessert?"

Pearl laughed. "Now, you know I always have room for dessert." She reached for her glass and took a sip of water. "You're going to have Thanksgiving dinner with us, right?"

Luther nodded. "Looking forward to it."

When their waiter arrived, Pearl and Luther placed orders for the pumpkin cheesecake.

"Are you going to the game tomorrow night?" Pearl asked.

"I'll be out of town for a meeting. I leave tonight for San Francisco. I'll be watching it on television though."

"I had to switch shifts with a coworker so that I could go. I didn't want to miss it."

"My dad once told me when Aunt Crystal was pregnant with you, your father was convinced that you were a boy, so he went out and bought you a basketball before you were born."

"I loved that basketball," Pearl murmured. "I remember when Daddy taught me how to dribble. I think I was about five or six. We had such a good time with him. And not enough with Mama. I wish they were both still here with us."

Luther nodded in understanding.

Their desserts arrived.

Pearl dived into her cheesecake. "Mmmm… this is delicious."

There was little conversation while they ate.

Pearl pulled her wallet out of her purse. "Thanks for having lunch with me."

"Keep your money," Luther said. "I'm paying."

"No, Luther, I invited you to lunch. This is my treat."

"Next time."

She smiled. "You say that all the time."

Luther paid the check and they left the restaurant.

Pearl gave him a hug. "It's so good seeing you. Safe travel to San Francisco."

He embraced her and kissed her on the cheek. "I'll call you when I get back."

They went in opposite directions upon leaving the parking lot. Pearl headed home to take a short nap before having to work the dinner shift.

Her thoughts turned to Wade as she passed the exit she took to the church. A brief shiver rippled through her when she recalled how much fun she had showing him around Mackinac Island.

He wasn't as bad as she first imagined, Pearl decided with a smile.

But was he the Mr. Right she spoke of?

Pearl was crushed. She shuddered inwardly just at the thought.

The Chargers lost to San Antonio by a mere two points.

Pearl shook her head sadly, swallowing the despair in her throat. "I guess we should head out," she said to Paige. "Let's round up the family." Opal was at the game with D'marcus, and so was Amber, sitting in another section.

Her cell phone rang.

It was Amber. "Meet us at Sterling's Café."

"Okay. We're on our way." Pearl clicked off. After a home game, it was their routine to meet at the café or one of the other restaurants located inside The Palace of Auburn Hills.

"Isn't that Pastor up ahead of us?" Paige asked, standing on tiptoe.

Pearl followed her gaze. "Yeah, that's him." They actually had something in common.

Unbelievable.

After walking into the lobby area, she speeded up, hoping to catch Wade before he had a chance to leave. "C'mon, Paige. Hurry up."

"What's the rush?"

"I want to say hello to Pastor."

"Why do I need to rush? You want to talk to him, not me."

Pearl took her cousin by the hand. "I don't want him to think anything other than we just bumped into him."

He was a few yards away, spurring her to walk a little faster. She wanted to catch Wade before he made it to the exit.

"Hello, Pastor," Pearl said as she tapped him on the shoulder.

Wade turned around, facing them. "Hello, ladies. Did you enjoy the game?"

Ignoring his formal tone, Pearl confessed, "I would've enjoyed it a lot more if we'd won."

She glanced over at Paige, silently urging her to say something.

Anything.

Her cousin caught the hint. "We didn't know you liked basketball, Pastor."

"It's one of my favorite sports," he replied.

Pearl was relieved when she glimpsed Opal, D'marcus and Amber walking toward them.

"Did you meet D'marcus Armstrong at the reunion?" she asked when the trio joined them.

He nodded. "It's good to see you again, Mr. Armstrong. The Chargers played well tonight."

"That's all anyone can ask. We were about to grab some coffee at Sterling's Café. Care to join us, Pastor?" D'marcus asked.

Checking his watch, Wade answered, "I can stay for one cup of coffee."

Pearl glanced over at Opal and Paige. They were grinning from ear to ear. "Don't start," she mouthed.

They sat down at one of the tables near the door, and D'marcus struck up a conversation with Wade while Opal and Amber sat on both sides of Pearl, wearing silly grins on their faces.

Wade's eyes landed on Pearl. His gaze was so penetrating, it sent a tremor through her body. She took a sip of her mocha latte.

"Did Pearl tell you that she's shopping her demo to record companies?" Amber blurted.

"No," Wade responded. "I had no idea. What type of music is it?"

"Gospel," Pearl replied. "Music is my ministry, Pastor."

"Is it traditional gospel music or that other stuff that's going around?"

Pearl sat up in her chair. Leaning forward, she asked, "What exactly do you mean by the 'other stuff that's going around'? Do you mean *contemporary* gospel music?"

Opal silently implored her to just let it go.

"Some of that stuff is not gospel music, you know that. Just because you throw God up in it doesn't make it gospel."

"I totally disagree with you," Pearl stated. "I don't think you should make a judgment call like that. You don't know the heart that's behind the song."

"Why don't we change the subject?" Opal suggested.

Pearl ignored her. "Look, Pastor Kendrick, just because you're old-fashioned doesn't mean everybody else has to live that way. I like the contemporary music and I like some of the more traditional songs, too."

"I'm not saying all contemporary music is bad. In fact, I'm not saying any of it is bad, per se. I just think that people have to make a choice. You're either going to sing to glorify the Lord or sing for people."

"You're saying that you can't do both, then?"

Wade met her gaze straight on. "It's called straddling the fence. You can't serve God and man both."

Pearl settled back in her chair. "Opal's right. We should talk about something else."

Whatever had made her wonder if Wade Kendrick could be Mr. Right? He was nothing but a jerk.

Chapter 6

Pearl Lockhart had never met an opinion she could keep to herself.

Wade left shortly after their little debate because he didn't want to make the others any more uncomfortable than they already were.

At home he slipped into a pair of pajamas and went through his nightly ritual. After relaxing in the living room for an hour he headed off to the bathroom. Reaching into the medicine cabinet, he pulled out a small bottle of pills and removed the white cap.

I need to get off this medication, he thought to himself.

He stared at the tiny white pill in the palm of his hand. He'd been taking one of them every night for the past ten years. He'd been diagnosed with chronic insomnia not too long after Jeff's death, but Wade knew it ran much deeper than that. This sleep aid kept his dreams from haunting him.

They weren't bad dreams or nightmares, but Wade didn't want to dream. Even in sleep, he couldn't face his father or his brother. He was too ashamed, too guilty.

Wade waited until he was sitting up in bed before he swallowed the pill. following it up with a glass of water. He picked up the novel he'd been reading. He would read until the tiny pill induced him to a full seven hours of dreamless sleep.

Two pages later, Wade began to feel the effects of the pill. He laid the book on the nightstand, settled down in bed and closed his eyes.

When he opened them again, it was almost 6:30 a.m.

Wade jumped out of bed to spend quality time with God. He prayed before reading several Bible passages.

After he showered, his stomach growled, signaling that it was time for breakfast. The bowl of cereal he ate after dressing didn't satisfy his hunger. It was times like this that he wished for a wife—one who could really throw down when it came to cooking.

Wade got to Lakeview Baptist Church at nine-thirty. He liked to be in his office no later than ten o'clock and always tried to leave around the same time each evening unless there was something special going on.

Though he had a great support staff, Wade had always been a "hands on" person, so he was around a lot more than it was assumed he would be. That was one of the complaints about the last pastor. He only worked one or two days a week and was never around when members wanted to meet with him.

Wade walked briskly through the doors of the administration building. Barbara had a cup of steaming coffee waiting for him.

"Good morning, Pastor," she greeted with a smile.

"Barbara, good morning. Thank you for the coffee."

"I made it just the way you like it. Two sugars and two teaspoons of French vanilla cream."

"I appreciate it." Wade headed to his office.

"What time is Phyllis coming in?" he asked, referring to the bookkeeper.

"She called and said she'll be here around eleven. She had to go to her son's school for a conference."

Wade nodded. "Would you let her know that I need to speak with her?"

"Of course, Pastor. As soon as she gets here."

"Thank you." Wade headed down the hall to his corner office.

The first thing he did was check his e-mail. He'd been invited to speak at a church in Los Angeles in January and was checking to see if he'd received the confirmation.

An image of Pearl unexpectedly appeared in his mind, distracting him.

Wade shook his head as if trying to shake her from his thoughts. He put a hand to his mouth, disconcerted.

He tried to regain his focus. Pearl was a distraction he could not afford but he couldn't escape the vision of the way she looked when he last saw her. Her hair, flowing free from chemicals and straightening combs, hung around her face, which had no makeup hiding her smooth complexion. She had worn a Detroit Chargers jersey over a pair of jeans that didn't take away from her femininity.

This is crazy. I can't start thinking about Pearl Lockhart like this.

Wade pushed away from his desk and went to the door. "Barbara, could you come here, please?"

His secretary yelled back, "I'll be right there."

Wade walked back over to his desk and sat down.

Barbara rushed in. "Sorry about that, Pastor. I was making an appointment for Iris Harrell's daughter. She's engaged and wants you to perform the ceremony."

"Did she sign up for the premarriage counseling sessions?"

"No. She just wants you to marry them."

His gaze met Barbara's. "Anyone wishing to get married here at Lakeview Baptist must attend the premarriage counseling sessions."

"They've been members of this church a long time, Pastor."

"I'm aware of that," Wade responded. "But the sessions are mandatory. They will enable engaged couples to enter marriage with greater understanding and certainty, which in turn will promote stability in their marriage."

She gave a stiff nod. "What did you need, Pastor?"

"I just wanted to know if the new member certificates were in. We need to have them ready this Sunday."

"They came in yesterday," Barbara responded. "I'll work on them this afternoon."

"If Sister Iris or her daughter has a problem with what I've said, I'd be more than happy to meet with them."

"I'm sure you'll be seeing them," she huffed.

Wade bit back a smile. "That will be all, Barbara."

She left the room, leaving him to ponder why it seemed he was on the road to making a lot of enemies within the congregation. Wade was only trying to take Lakeview Baptist Church to the next level.

When Wade answered the call to preach, he promised God that he would follow the laws of the Bible and that any church that he accepted leadership over would do the same.

God would hold him accountable for his actions. This time he vowed not to treat his responsibility lightly.

Pearl switched her cellular phone to her other ear. "Ruby, when are you making the sweet potato pies?" she asked while strolling down the vegetable aisle in the grocery store. "I can pick up the stuff now. I'm in the store."

"I have most of what I need," her sister responded. "I'll be doing my shopping this weekend. Hey, can you make the macaroni and cheese?"

Pearl eyed the fresh broccoli for a moment before moving on. "Ruby, the last time I made the macaroni and cheese it turned out horribly. Too much of one thing and not enough of the other. Tell Opal to make it. She makes great mac and cheese."

"So what are you going to make?" Ruby inquired.

"I'm going to make the green-bean casserole and the lemon pound cake I make every year. Paige is making her famous red-velvet cake." After a brief pause she added, "Thanksgiving is ten days away. We still have a lot of time. Stop worrying. We do this every year and it always comes out just right."

Pearl ended her phone call so that she could concentrate on her shopping.

Six plastic bags later, she pushed her shopping cart out of the store.

Amber and Paige were in the living room talking when Pearl arrived home.

"Need some help?" her sister offered.

"This is all of it," Pearl responded. She removed the bags from the folding grocery cart then went in to hug Amber. "I didn't know you were coming over. I figured you had enough of us last night at the game."

"I was driving by and before I knew it, I was parking the car in front of your building."

Pearl embraced her cousin. "Hey, roomie."

"Hey, girl."

Amber and Paige helped Pearl put away the groceries.

"How long is that gorgeous Dashuan Kennedy going to be on suspension?" Amber asked. "That man needs to be in the game, not sitting on the bench."

"Why?" Pearl questioned. "He's nothing but trouble, Amber. Just talk to D'marcus if you don't believe me. He'll tell you the same thing."

"Pearl's right," Paige interjected. "Lyman told me that Dashuan is a womanizer and that he's running around with Kelvin Landy. You know, they say that Kelvin hangs with some rough people."

"That's just a rumor," Amber argued. "The only

thing we really know about Kelvin is that he's a physical therapist. He's been working with Dashuan since he hurt his knee. Kelvin works with the Chargers. If he was so bad, why wouldn't D'marcus or the other owners get rid of him?"

Pearl eyed her sister. "How do you know so much about Dashuan and Kelvin? You've never met either one as far as I know."

"D'marcus owns the Chargers—did you forget? I've been doing some research."

"Amber, don't even waste your time. Dashuan is not your type. He's trouble." Pearl put away the last item in the refrigerator. "You can do a whole lot better than him."

She could tell by the way Amber stood with her arms folded across her chest, rolling her eyes, that her sister wasn't listening. Amber was twenty-one and didn't want any of her siblings trying to tell her how to live her life. At times Pearl felt the same way so she backed off. "You're smart. I know you'll make the right decision."

Amber gave her a grateful smile.

"Colleen and I went shopping yesterday," Amber said when they'd settled down in the living room. "You should see the leather dress she bought. It's sexy."

Paige sat up. "My sister actually bought a leather dress?"

Laughing, Amber nodded. "I have to admit that I talked her into it. You have to see it. It looks great on Colleen."

"I'm not surprised," Pearl stated. "Colleen has a nice body." She paused a moment before adding, "I'm so glad Opal changed her style. I love her new makeover. She looks so much younger."

"It's not that makeover that's got her glowing. It's that man. D'marcus Armstrong is why she's walking around with her head in the heavens." Paige grinned, running her fingers through her braids. "I know because Lyman's got me doing the same thing."

"Oh, stop bragging," Pearl complained. "Amber and I don't need to be reminded of how single we are."

The women laughed.

Amber stayed at the apartment with them until 10:00 p.m. Yawning, she stood up and said, "I need to get home." She fingered her long, honey-blond curls. "Give me a call tomorrow, Pearl. Let's try to meet up for lunch or for some shopping."

"I'm working the lunch shift but I'll be off around four."

Amber strolled over to the front door. "Better yet, let's meet at Image Nails." Her mouth thinned with displeasure. "You need to get your eyebrows waxed."

"I love you, too," Pearl responded. "Call us when you get home."

"I will," she said. Amber opened the door and walked out.

"Amber wants Lyman to introduce her to Dashuan," Paige announced. "I don't think it's a good idea."

"Don't do it," Pearl stated with a shake of her head.

"She'll just ask Lyman herself. Or D'marcus."

"D'marcus is not going to introduce Amber to that jerk. He can barely stand the man himself. Plus, he's not going to risk Opal getting mad at him."

"She's such a beautiful girl," Pearl said with a soft sigh. "I just wish she'd use the brains God gave her."

"She's so man-crazy."

Pearl agreed. "Amber still needs to use wisdom. She thinks she knows everything but she just doesn't know the half of it."

"Hmm…sounds like another girl I know. Miss 'Wishing on a Star' Lockhart."

Laughing, Pearl tossed a pillow at her cousin.

Thursday evening, Pearl met with the youth for choir rehearsal. She sat at the piano playing softly as the teens filtered in. One of the girls approached her.

"Miss Pearl, you rocking that outfit."

Grinning, she responded, "Girl, am I really rocking it?"

"It's tight. I like that. You was rocking that leather skirt, too."

Pearl didn't even want to think back to the way she embarrassed herself. Eying the girl standing beside her, she said, "Veronica, you're looking pretty sharp yourself. I'm gonna have to see if they make those jeans in my size."

"Miss Pearl, you not that much bigger than me," Veronica responded with a laugh.

More choir members arrived.

Pearl stopped playing the piano and stood up. She made her way over to the front of the choir stand. "Hello, everybody," she greeted. "Did you have a good day today?"

There were a few nods and a couple of no's.

"C'mon now, I know something good happened to each of you today. What's the first thing you should be thankful for?"

"For waking up," they said in unison.

"If you woke up in your right mind and with your health, give God some praise." Pearl began clapping her hands. "C'mon, give Him praise. We are to praise the Lord in good times and bad."

Applause filled the sanctuary.

"Before we praise God in song, who would like to lead us in prayer?" Pearl inquired.

Veronica volunteered.

Pearl closed her eyes as Veronica began to pray.

Afterwards, she said, "Has anyone talked to Tyson?"

Tyson was thirteen years old and the son of one of her close friends. Pearl was a little worried about him since finding some drawings of gang symbols in his backpack.

"I haven't talked to him in a couple of days," one of the boys responded.

"Okay, well, let's get started. Everybody stand up. The first thing we need to do is our warm-up exercises. Veronica, could you lead them, please?"

Pearl went over to a young man sitting at the piano. She gave him the arrangements for the new song they were about to practice. "I made a few changes," she whispered. Pointing, she added, "Right here."

As they sang Pearl kept checking over her

shoulder just in case Tyson had slipped inside. It wasn't like him to miss practice.

"Let's go over it one more time," Pearl said. "You did a wonderful job, but if we're going to sing this song on the fourth Sunday, let's rehearse it one more time. We're not having choir rehearsal next Thursday because it'll be Thanksgiving."

Loud groans from the teenagers were heard throughout the choir stand, sparking a chuckle from Pearl. "C'mon y'all. Don't give me a hard time."

Pearl gestured for the pianist to start playing.

The group went over the song once more. Pearl clapped when they finished. "Beautiful," she complimented. "You guys did a wonderful job."

She had the choir run through one more song.

Pearl had just called rehearsal to a close when a boy walked inside the sanctuary. She glanced over her shoulder saying, "Tyson, you're late. Choir practice is pretty much over."

"I just came by to tell you that I'm not singing in the choir no more."

She turned around to face him. "Why not?"

"It's whack."

Pearl surveyed the teen's face. "Does your mother know about your plans, Tyson?" Her friend, Yolanda, would have a fit if she knew her son was trying to leave the choir.

"This is my life," he stated. "I can do whatever I want. Can't nobody make me stay if I don't want to sing."

"I don't believe your mother would agree. In fact, I think she'd have a problem with all of this."

He shrugged in nonchalance.

"Do me a favor and hang around, Tyson. I'd like to talk to you."

"Miss Pearl…"

"Don't you go anywhere, Tyson," she told him firmly. "I mean it. We need to talk." Pearl turned her attention to a couple of teens who were waiting to speak with her.

Out the corner of her eye, she noticed Wade standing in the side door. *How long has he been there?* she wondered.

After the teens left, Pearl returned to Tyson. "Your mother and I are very worried about you. She told me you were failing some of your classes. Tyson, that's not like you."

He didn't respond, just dropped down on the front pew looking sullen.

"Your mother loves you very much. So do I.

Sweetie, I've known you since the day you were born. You're like my own child."

"I ain't doing nothin', Miss Pearl. G-Dog and I...we just hanging."

Wade walked over to where they were sitting.

"Good evening."

"Hello, Pastor." Pearl gave him a tiny smile. "I know we ran a little late tonight, but we're on our way out."

"I'd like to speak to you, if you have a moment."

She was keenly aware of his scrutiny. "Sure." To Tyson, she said, "Hon, this won't take long."

He released a long sigh and muttered something under his breath, then walked to the back and sat down in the last row.

Normally, Pearl would've called Tyson on it, but she decided to let it go this one time. Right now she was trying to figure out why Wade wanted to talk to her.

She and Wade walked back up to the front of the church and sat down on the first pew.

"I won't keep you long."

"It's not a problem. What can I do for you?"

"I was listening to some of the songs that you're planning to have the youth choir sing on fourth

Sunday. While they're nice, I'd really like you to add some of the more traditional songs to your list."

Keeping her expression under stern restraint, Pearl eyed him. "Okay, so now you have a problem with the songs I choose for the choir to sing?" Shaking her head in dismay, she added, "I don't believe you, Pastor."

Why did Pearl always have to be so defensive? It was a simple request.

Wade chose his words carefully. "I'm not saying anything is wrong with them, per se. I just think that some people have forgotten that the primary focus should be bringing people to Christ, while being an example of what they are singing about."

"I see." Just when she thought he was beginning to relax…

"I take it that you don't agree."

"It's not that I don't agree, Pastor. I happen to believe that every song the youth choir sings accomplishes just that. I wrote quite a few of those songs."

Pearl glanced over her shoulder to where Tyson was sitting. "Before I took over the choir we barely had any young people in the church, much less the choir. We need music that will reach these kids."

Wade had overheard her conversation with Tyson. It was clear to him just how much she cared about the teen, as well as all the youth at Lakeview Baptist Church. The girls looked up to her and the boys thought she was fine.

He smiled. They were right. There was no denying that.

Tyson stood up abruptly. "Miss Pearl, I need to get home. You ain't gotta drive me to the house. My friend's waiting on me outside."

Pearl turned around. "Then you can tell him to leave because I'm taking you home. I want to talk to you," she insisted.

"I told you, Miss Pearl. I'm not doing nothing, so you don't have to worry 'bout me."

"Well, I do," she countered. "Especially since I saw those drawings in your backpack. I wasn't prying. I found the backpack in the choir stand and only wanted to see who it belonged to."

"I'm going straight home, Miss Pearl."

"I'm driving you and that's final."

"Actually, I'd like to take Tyson home," Wade interjected, surprising both Pearl and Tyson.

The teen sighed loudly before saying, "Mama called you. Didn't she?"

Nodding, Wade answered, "She's very concerned about you."

Pearl sent him a smile of gratitude. "Thanks so much for this," she whispered as they walked toward the exit doors. "I know he's been running around with some gang members." After a short pause, she added, "I just hate that. All being part of a gang can do is get you killed."

Wade stiffened at her words.

He escorted Tyson and Pearl out of the church.

"Hey, man, what took you so long?" another teenage boy said when Tyson stepped out.

Tyson glanced over at Pearl.

"Hello," Wade said to the boy. "I'm Pastor Kendrick. What's your name, young man?"

The boy looked from Wade to Tyson, then back to Wade. "G-Dog," he muttered warily. His eyes were sharp and assessing.

"It's nice to meet you, G-Dog," Wade stated sincerely, and offered his hand, which the teen shook.

"I know you were waiting on Tyson to come out, but I'm going to drive him home because his mother wants me to talk to him. I'd be more than happy to give you a ride, as well."

G-Dog shook his head. 'I'm all right." He turned to walk away, then paused. "Hey, Pastor, thanks."

Wade nodded. "You're welcome."

He unlocked his car door and gestured for Tyson to get inside. Wade then escorted Pearl to her SUV.

"Wow," Pearl murmured. "You really handled that G-Dog well. I thought he'd give you a lot more attitude. I didn't know if he was going to pull out a gun or something."

"Gang members want respect. They want that more than anything else."

Pearl eyed him. "You seem to know a lot about this. Maybe you should meet with the teens at church to discuss gangs."

Wade didn't respond.

Pearl pulled a CD out of her tote. Offering it out to Wade, she said, "Here…I want you to listen to this. I wrote all of the songs."

"I look forward to listening to it."

"After you hear it, I think you'll understand what I've been trying to tell you."

Wade waited until Pearl climbed into her car. "Drive safe," he told her.

Her compelling eyes held him captive, prolonging the moment. "You do the same."

Pearl waved before pulling off. She left the parking lot and disappeared into the night.

"What did my mom want you to talk to me about?" Tyson asked when Wade got into his car.

"She's worried about certain choices you've been making. She says your grades are dropping since you started hanging with G-Dog and his boys."

"They don't have anything to do with my grades."

Wade pulled out into traffic and glanced over at Tyson. "Then why don't you tell me what's going on with you?"

His gray eyes became flat and unreadable as stone. "Nothing's going on."

"Tyson, you can tell me anything. I won't judge you."

"I'm just having some problems with my school work, that's all. G-Dog is my friend. I'm not in a gang like everybody thinks."

"Then why are you running around with gang members?"

"They're my friends. In a way, I think it's cool because nobody will mess with them, but..." Tyson's voice died.

"But what?" Wade prompted.

"Some of the stuff I hear about scares me. G-Dog's big brother...he's the leader."

"G-Dog's in the gang because of his brother?" Wade asked.

Tyson nodded. "Yeah. He don't want King to think he a punk."

Back in Wade's mind, he wondered if that's why Jeff wanted to be part of the Chicago Kings. Clearing his throat, he said, "That's not a good reason to join. You do realize that, don't you?"

"G-Dog makes it sound cool sometimes."

"That's because he's trying to recruit you, Tyson."

Wade hoped that his words were seeping into Tyson's head. "This is not the route you want to take," he told the teen. "Gang violence is on the rise."

"That's not what the Detroit Disciples are about, Pastor."

"What makes them different from any of the other gangs out there?"

Tyson sighed in frustration. "You don't understand, Pastor."

Wade understood. He understood more than Tyson knew. "It's not cool, Tyson. Trust me. What's so cool about tagging and stealing? That's the way boys your age prove you're worthy of belonging."

Tyson sighed. "It ain't like that, Pastor. I don't mean no disrespect but how do you know what happens in gangs? You ain't never been in one. The Disciples—they just trying to help the community."

Wade held his tongue. He couldn't tell Tyson about Jeff, about his former life. It just wasn't something he could talk about right now.

"My house is the first one on the left," Tyson instructed.

Wade pulled in front of a modest brick home and parked the car.

Tyson got out and walked as slow as he could to the front door. Wade strode beside him.

The boy's mother was waiting for him in the living room. She greeted Wade, and then lit into her son. "Pearl called me and told me that you quit the choir. You're not quitting so just take that thought out of your head right this minute."

Tyson's eyes were glued to the shag carpet. He dropped down on the sofa.

"I told you I didn't want you hanging around with that G-Dog. He ain't nothing but trouble," she fumed.

He continued to defend G-Dog. "He ain't trying to force me to do anything I don't want to do."

"He's a gangbanger," she countered. "I'm telling you the truth. That boy means you no good."

"He can't make me do nothing I don't want to do."

"Well, you'd better not be wanting to join a gang. That's all I got to say on the matter and that's final."

Wade decided now was a good time to intervene. "Tyson and I had a talk on the way over, Sister Yolanda. He assured me that he isn't in the gang."

"She don't believe me," Tyson complained. "Just 'cause me and G-Dog friends don't mean I want to be part of the Disciples. Even though they treat me better than *she* does."

"Excuse me? Do they feed you?" Yolanda demanded. "Do they buy the clothes you're wearing? What do they do for you, Tyson Terrell Washington?"

"They don't ask me where I'm going all the time. They don't tell me what I can or can't do. They treat me like a man."

"They are not your mother," she countered. "But I am. I'm not trying to hurt you or get you killed. Son, I love you more than my own life. It is not my job to be anything other than your parent. I take my role seriously and as long as I have breath in my body you ain't joining the Disciples or anybody else. Do you understand me, Tyson?"

Wade remembered all too well having those same conversations with his mother. How he wished he could go back in time and change the choices he made, but that's not what life was about. It was learning from past mistakes. He didn't want Tyson to have to go through life living with guilt.

Wade stayed another fifteen minutes to try and get Tyson to listen and consider everything his mother was telling him. He said a prayer and bid Yolanda and Tyson a good night.

His heart was troubled because Wade wasn't sure he'd been able to reach the teen at all. But he also felt guilty. He wasn't man enough to share his own experiences. Wade didn't want to see another person look at him with disappointment.

He especially never wanted Pearl to see him as a gangbanger who ended up getting his brother killed.

His faith in God was strong, and while Wade knew deep down that God had forgiven him, he still had no peace. He'd let his family down when they needed him the most. The guilt of his actions had seeped into his pores for all eternity.

Chapter 7

Wade slipped Pearl's CD in the compact disc player as soon as he walked into his house. He loved listening to her sing and was impressed by Pearl's music and the fact that her words really ministered to his soul.

Her music reminded him of soft jazz but the words were unmistakable. Pearl's lyrics seeped into his spirit. Leaning back against the sofa, Wade closed his eyes and imagined himself before the Lord, praising him.

The next day, he was surprised to run into Pearl at the bookstore.

"Wade...hello."

He eyed the stack of music in her hands. "Looking for some new songs for the youth choir?"

"Naaah. This is for the fashion show." Pearl was the coordinator for the annual youth luncheon. This year the event was going to be held on the Saturday after Thanksgiving.

"I have to tell you I enjoyed listening to your CD. The lyrics really ministered to me. I have to admit that you were right about *your* music. I still have a problem with some of the stuff that's masquerading as gospel music."

"I'm thankful you listened with an open mind," responded Pearl. "I get what you were saying about some of the music out there, but, Pastor, there are some wonderful contemporary artists who are using their gifts to minister to the non-Christian or the unchurched."

"The idea that ministry must get out by any means necessary is pervasive to me. For whatever reason, some people have this preconceived notion that we have to change the music in order to reach a larger number of people—"

Pearl quickly interjected, "Who otherwise wouldn't step foot into a church."

Shifting in her seat, she added, "Contemporary music adds that edge that more traditional music doesn't. People can relate to it and the words minister to them."

"So what you're telling me is that only the new and improved music will save souls?" Wade asked. "That the more traditional music won't work anymore?"

"That's not what I'm saying at all. I just believe you have to meet people where they are. My own spiritual walk was not reflected in any of the traditional songs. They didn't do anything for me, honestly. You may not know this but we didn't have a youth choir until I took over," Pearl stated. "And we don't just sing contemporary songs. I try to balance it out with some traditional ones."

"I know you do, Pearl. I'm just suggesting to maybe add more traditional music. I don't mind you singing one contemporary song during service. I don't want people coming just to be entertained. We are here to minister."

Folding her arms across her chest, Pearl questioned, "Are you trying to tell me what to sing? Would you like to listen to these?" she asked, holding out the CDs. "See if they meet with your approval?"

"I don't think I need to do that."

"I was being sarcastic, Wade."

"So was I," he responded. "Pearl, I was only making a suggestion."

"Thank you for your suggestion. I'll give it some thought."

Pearl walked up to the counter to pay for her purchases, Wade on her heels.

"I'll take care of this," he told her. "They're for a church function."

"You don't have to d—"

He cut her off, saying, "I insist."

"Thank you," Pearl said after a moment.

"You're welcome." Handing her the bag containing the music CDs, Wade eyed her as they made their way out of the store. "You're very different from how I assumed you were."

`Giving him a sidelong glance, she asked, "Do I even want to know what your impression was of me?"

He laughed. "No. Probably not."

"Pastor, there's something I need from you," Pearl stated.

"What is it?"

"Your trust. If you want me to continue as your youth-choir director, I really need you to trust me and my choices in songs. I want these kids to sing their hearts out. I want them to sing with joy before the Lord. But mostly I want them to be able to relate to what they're singing."

Wade nodded in understanding. "I will allow you to do your job."

"Thank you." After a brief pause, Pearl inquired, "Do you have plans for dinner, Pastor?"

"Actually, I don't."

"We have a new item on the menu at Milton's— a sautéed salmon. I'm sure you'd like it. Think about it," she murmured. "I'm working the dinner shift."

With that, she walked away.

Wade watched her go, stunned. After a moment he smiled. Just like he'd said, Sister Pearl was full of surprises.

Wade followed the hostess to the back of the restaurant where Pearl was working. He kept telling himself that it was his growling stomach that brought him back to Milton's Ristorante, but deep down, he knew better.

He wanted to see Pearl.

Pearl broke into a big grin when she saw him. "Glad you decided to join us tonight."

"Glad you invited me," he responded.

"You won't be disappointed." Pearl pulled out her pad of paper.

"So are you going to try the salmon scaloppini?"

"It's between the shrimp al arrabiata and the salmon." Wade laid down his menu. "I think I'll let you decide for me."

"Do you like spicy foods?"

"Some…not a lot."

"Then you should definitely stick with the salmon."

"I trust you."

Their gaze met and held for a moment. He wondered if she caught the deeper meaning to his words.

Pearl seemed to be the one to recover first. "I'll go put your order in."

Wade watched her until he could no longer see her.

What am I doing here?

He was attracted to Pearl. Wade still had trouble digesting this particular fact. She was the total opposite of the type of women he'd dated in the past.

Pearl checked on him twice before she returned with his food. He noted she was just as attentive to all of her customers. Her smile was infectious and had a soothing effect on everyone. Except him, he realized. When she smiled at him, his heart beat faster.

"So what did you think of the salmon?" she asked, suddenly appearing at his table.

"Pearl, you were right. It was delicious."

She broke into a wide grin. "I told you."

"Thanks. You saved me from a peanut-butter-and-jelly sandwich for dinner tonight."

"Oh, my."

"Cooking is not one of my talents, unfortunately."

"I'm surprised," she murmured. "You look like you can do everything well." Pearl cleared her throat softly before adding, "I need to check on my other tables."

Wade chuckled.

When she returned to his table with his bill, he slipped cash into the padfolio, leaving her a very generous tip. Then he sought out the bathroom.

When Wade walked out of the men's room, Pearl was clocking out. "You're off work?" he inquired.

She nodded. "Yeah, and I have to tell you I'm so glad. I'm tired."

"It's too bad you're tired. I was thinking about seeing a movie. I thought maybe you could join me?"

Pearl broke into a grin. "Sure. I'm in the mood for a movie."

"Great. Do you want to leave your car here and ride with me?"

"I'll just freshen up here and meet you at the movieplex."

"I'll wait here and you can follow me over."

She nodded. "I'll only be a minute. I keep some clothes in my locker."

In minutes Pearl met Wade by the front door. She'd exchanged her white shirt for a jade-green sweater.

"Ready?"

He gave a slight nod. "Let's go."

Wade escorted Pearl to her car, then went to his. She followed him a couple of blocks to the movie theater.

What am I doing? Wade wondered to himself the entire drive over, and now as he stood in the lobby with Pearl.

"You're awfully quiet," she said, breaking into his thoughts.

"I'm sorry. I didn't mean to be rude."

Pearl surprised him by laughing. "You know, we're acting like a couple of nervous kids."

Wade chuckled. "You're right."

"We're just two people here to watch a movie," Pearl stated. "We won't be talking so there's minimal risk of arguing or debating. Surely, we can handle that."

"I know I can. But can *you?*"

She glanced up at him. "Yeah. I can do this."

Wade laughed, the tension leaving his body. Pearl loved life and he admired her zest. He settled back in his seat to enjoy the movie.

Two and a half hours later, they emerged from the theater.

Wade gestured toward the ice-cream parlor in the next block. "Interested?"

"Sure," Pearl answered.

A few minutes later, they sat in one of the booths eating ice cream.

"I'm going to have to do another mile on the treadmill," announced Pearl. "I don't mind though. I haven't had an ice-cream sundae this good in a while."

"Do you work out on a regular basis?"

"I try to exercise every day but sometimes I can't. What about you? What do you do to keep yourself looking good?"

"I work out at least three days a week. I have

some equipment at home so I'm on it whenever I have a moment."

Pearl checked her watch. "Can you believe it? We haven't disagreed once."

"We've had other moments like this. We didn't argue at the wedding reception."

"That's right. Or after the basketball game. We're starting a trend."

He laughed. "I like you, Pearl Lockhart."

"I like you, too, Wade. You're an okay guy. You just need to lighten up some. Not be so stuffy."

"I'll take your suggestion under advisement."

Paige and Pearl left the apartment early to get to the nail salon.

"You got in late last night," Paige said as they waited for their turn. "I thought you were getting off early."

"Wade came to the restaurant for dinner. He and I went to see a movie afterward."

"Oh, really?"

"Don't even go there," Pearl warned. "It wasn't a date."

"You don't have to keep secrets from me."

"I'm not keeping any secrets, Paige. Wade and

I…we're getting to know one another. That's it. If anything, we'll become friends."

After the manicure and pedicure, Pearl and her cousin parted ways. She had to work the lunch shift.

The restaurant was already crowded by the time she arrived. Pearl didn't waste any time. She clocked in and headed off to her station, humming to the music filtering through the sound system overhead.

A couple of her friends showed up and were seated in her station, but it was Ruby who surprised her.

"I didn't expect to see you here."

"I was downtown for a meeting, so I thought I'd have lunch here." Ruby studied the menu, then laid it down. "So what's going on with you?"

"Not a thing," Pearl responded with a chuckle. "Still waiting to get the recording contract. I haven't gotten any rejections yet, so I'm still hopeful."

Ruby nodded. She studied Pearl's face. "You look really happy. Happier than usual. Any reason?"

"No," Pearl said, shaking her head. "Today is just a good day."

She was so busy that four o'clock rolled around before Pearl even realized. She was thrilled to be clocking out, and was looking forward to enjoying the rest of her day just doing something she liked instead of working.

Just as she was leaving, she ran into Wade.

"Can't get enough of this place?" Pearl inquired.

"I'm picking up a take-out order. It's your fault, you know. You got me started on the salmon."

She broke into a grin. "I've created a monster, I see."

"Are you leaving?"

Nodding, she replied, "I'm off work."

"Have you eaten anything?"

"Not since breakfast. I was busy from the minute I walked into this place."

"Why don't you join me?" he asked, surprising Pearl. "I was planning on take-out but I can eat here."

She jumped at the opportunity to spend more time with Wade. "Just let me change my shirt. Go on and have Myra seat you. I'll meet you at the table."

Pearl wasn't gone long.

When she returned, Pearl said, "I think you know a whole lot more about me than I know about you. If you were listening at the reunion, you know most of my family's history. Wade, tell me about yourself. I'd like to get to know the real you."

He shrugged. "Not much to tell."

"What did you do as a child? Did you play any sports?"

"I played basketball for a while. I stopped when my dad died."

"Why?"

"I had to look after my younger brother while my mom worked."

"You became the man of the house, I guess."

He took a sip of his water, then said, "I did what I thought was best at the time."

"Do you have any other brothers or sisters?"

"No. There was just the two of us." Wade took a long drink of water.

"So where does your brother live? Is he still in Gary?"

"My family remained in Chicago. I left when I was eighteen. Right after my brother died."

"Oh, I'm sorry."

Wade abruptly changed the subject. "It was a pretty nice day today. Did you get to enjoy any of it?"

"Actually, I did," Pearl answered. "Paige and I spent the morning getting manicures and pedicures." Grinning, she added, "We ladies have to pamper ourselves every now and then."

"I suppose we men have to do the same."

"So what do you do to pamper yourself, Wade?" Pearl asked after the waitress took their orders.

"I sit around and do nothing."

Leaning forward, Pearl asked, "Are you serious?"

"Yeah. I'm always on the go, so when I have time to just sit down and relax, that's a luxury."

"Next time I go for a massage I need to take you with me. You need one."

"Why do you say that?"

"I'm not so sure you really know how to relax. Doing nothing is okay, but are you really in a relaxed state? Or is your mind still running a mile a minute?"

"I guess you have a point. I do think a lot."

"Wade, you need to free your mind. Sometimes I meditate. I lock myself in my room, put on some soft jazz and just imagine myself off on a beach somewhere. Paradise."

"That sounds nice."

"You're welcome to share my beach with me. It's so beautiful and peaceful."

"Tell me more about it."

Leaning back in her chair, Pearl closed her eyes. "The ocean water is a clear, crystal blue. The sun is shining and the weather is perfect. Not too hot and not too cool. The sand...Wade, the sand is white and the trees are so green and beautiful. It's so serene."

"What does the air smell like?" he asked, images forming in his mind.

"Like jasmine."

"Jasmine?"

"I love jasmine. The island also has scores of exotic plants and flowers in every vibrant color imaginable."

"Your island does sound beautiful, Pearl."

"It relaxes me to imagine myself on the beach with no worries. I can exist there with no past or present."

"I like that," Wade said almost to himself. "No past or present."

She eyed him. "You're thinking about your brother and your father, aren't you? I know I miss my parents every day."

"Time is supposed to ease the pain, but it

doesn't really." Wade shook his head sadly. "There's so much I would've done differently."

"Like what? What would you have changed?"

"Let's talk about something a little less sobering."

"Okay, what should we talk about? I know. You can tell me what you thought about James Patterson's latest novel. I remember you telling me you were reading it. Did you like it?"

He nodded. "You like thrillers?"

"Love them is a more accurate description. James Patterson is my favorite author. That's why I asked. I haven't had a chance to read it yet."

"In my opinion, this one is his best work," Wade stated.

"It's hard to believe that as different as we are we have so much in common. Who would've thunk it?" Pearl asked playfully, glancing at him. "Did you ever think we'd become friends?" She wrenched herself away from her ridiculous preoccupation with his handsome face.

"Are we becoming friends?"

Wade's voice was so low that she had to strain to hear his question.

Pearl met his gaze, suddenly dark and smoldering. "I guess we'll just have to see where this road takes us."

Chapter 8

Wade hated for the evening to end because that meant he and Pearl would go their separate ways.

Pearl had such a warm, loving spirit and she was always smiling. He loved her sense of humor and the sense of freedom she seemed to have in her life. Not only was she beautiful but she was intelligent, as well. The more he got to know her, the more he wanted to know about her.

An undeniable magnetism was building between them, forcing him to acknowledge the truth. *I'm beginning to have real feelings for her.*

The silent declaration surprised him, but Wade didn't bother to deny the truth. There was not much point.

But as strong as his attraction was to Pearl, he would never act on those feelings. While they'd found some common ground, they still had very different views of what they wanted for the future.

A relationship between them could never work. She wanted to sing professionally while Wade was content leading the congregation of Lakeview Baptist. But still, their different goals didn't diminish his attraction.

Their time together drew to an end when the staff started cleaning up. Wade walked Pearl to her car and watched her drive off, silently wanting to call her back.

He pulled up the collar of his jacket and walked briskly to his car, driving home.

He tried watching television and reading, but he couldn't focus on either. Pearl was still at the forefront of his mind.

He was grateful when an hour later Harold called.

"Uncle Harold, how are you?"

"Doing fine. Just fine. Ivy and I just got back from Gary not too long ago. We went back for a birthday party." He lapsed into a recap of his visit.

"Cassie and her husband are coming to the house tomorrow to have dinner with us," Harold announced. "Why don't you join us if you're free?"

"I don't have any plans," Wade responded. "But I'll call you tomorrow after church to confirm."

Wade ended the call a few seconds later.

He went through his nightly ritual of reading his Bible and saying his prayers before settling down in bed.

His last thoughts before falling asleep were of Pearl and how much he'd relished the time he spent with her. His feelings for her were beginning to deepen.

Was he falling in love with her?

When service ended on Sunday, Pearl came over to say hello. "I really enjoyed your sermon this morning."

Wade smiled. "Thank you." He couldn't resist adding, "This means a lot coming from you."

Pearl laughed. She stole a peek over her shoulder before saying, "I know this is really last minute, but would you be interested in seeing the Chargers take on the Chicago Hawks? The game starts at six. Opal can't make it and we have an extra ticket." Pearl quickly added, "It's not a date or anything."

"Thanks for clearing that up," he teased.

"I didn't mean it like that. I just don't want to place you in an uncomfortable position."

"Pearl, I would love to go. Thank you."

"You're welcome. Your ticket will be at Will Call. See you tonight."

Pearl gave him a tiny smile then walked away. He watched her until she disappeared through the exit doors.

"Good afternoon, Pastor," a woman's voice greeted from behind him.

Wade turned around. "Sister Marnie. It's a blessing you could join us this Sunday."

"I'm working this evening, but I wanted to make sure I came this morning. I didn't want to miss you preaching. Pastor, I truly enjoyed the sermon. It spoke volumes to me."

He smiled politely.

"I'm planning on cooking a great big Thanksgiving dinner on Thursday. I'd love for you to join us. Unless you have other plans with some lucky lady."

Wade searched for the right words.

Marnie lowered her voice. "Pastor, I'm not very good at playing coy. I'm a straight shooter so I'm going to lay my cards on the table. Auntie's told me quite a bit about you and I really like what I've heard. You're the type of man that I'd be interested in getting to know better." She paused for a heartbeat before adding, "However, I don't like to waste my time. If you're not feeling me, just let me know. I'm a big girl. I can take it."

Wade chose his words carefully. "Sister Marnie, I'm flattered. You're a nice person and I think that you'll make some man very happy one day."

"But that man is not you," she interjected with a frown. "Is that what you're trying to tell me?"

"I'm afraid so. I hope I haven't offended you."

Shrugging, Marnie stated, "No, you haven't. It's your loss, Pastor. I know I'm a good catch and any man in his right mind would want to be with me. Someone else must have caught your eye. Perhaps the woman you were just talking to— Pearl Lockhart."

When he didn't respond, she murmured, "I wonder if she has any idea just what a lucky woman she is." Switching her purse from one shoulder to the other, Marnie gave a soft sigh of resignation. "Have a blessed week, Pastor. Happy Thanksgiving."

"Thank you, Sister Marnie. Same to you."

"One final word of advice, Pastor. If you want Miss Lockhart, you'd better move quick. She's a very beautiful woman and she doesn't strike me as the type who's just going to wait around for a man."

He smiled. "Thanks for the advice."

Watching Marnie walk away, Wade considered her words.

All three of her sisters and Paige were waiting for her by the Explorer when she walked out of the church. Pearl took her time walking across the parking lot.

"So, is Pastor going to the game with us?" Amber asked.

"No. He's going by himself," Pearl stated. "I told him that the ticket will be left at Will Call."

Ruby shook her head sadly.

"I never said I was going to ask the man on a date. Besides, the way I see it, you should have been the one to ask him," she said to Opal. "It was your ticket."

"He's going to be sitting with us, Pearl. You

could've made him feel just a little more welcome."

"Opal, if the man wants to go on a date, he should ask me on one. This isn't a big deal. Really. It was your idea to give him the ticket. I did that." Pearl unlocked her SUV, saying, "I'll see you later. I need to take care of some stuff before the game tonight."

She felt guilty for being so snippy with her sisters. She knew she was overly sensitive when it came to Wade.

Am I that transparent when it comes to him? she wondered silently.

She stole a peek in her rearview mirror.

Her sisters were still huddled together. Probably talking about her and Wade. Paige had walked over to her car and looked like she was getting ready to leave. Pearl shook her head. She loved her sisters dearly but they were so nosy.

When Pearl arrived home a couple of hours later, Paige was in her bedroom talking to Lyman on the telephone.

Pearl went to her own room. She had gone to the mall after leaving the church and purchased a pair of jeans and a sweater with the Charger team colors. She usually wore her team jersey, but with Wade joining them, she wanted to look her best.

As if he's going to care what I look like.

Pearl laid out her clothing, then went into the bathroom to style her hair. She tried several different looks before deciding on pulling her sandy brown mane back into a curly afro puff.

"You're working pretty hard for your nondate," Paige stated. "New outfit, new hairstyle."

"This has nothing to do with Wade. I'm doing all this for me."

"Liar."

Pearl turned around. "I wore the jersey to the last game. Okay."

"It's not like you haven't washed it. What's the big deal?"

"I want to wear something new, Paige. There's nothing wrong with that."

"There's nothing wrong with trying to look cute for Pastor, either."

Pearl broke into laughter. "Give it up."

She decided to ride over with Paige to The Palace of Auburn Hills. Pearl spotted Wade minutes after entering the Captain's Quarters restaurant that was located inside the facility.

"I see you made it," she said.

"Thanks again for the ticket," Wade said as he glanced around the restaurant. "VIP Section B.

Great seat. I was in the nosebleed section last time I was here. Why don't you let me pay you?"

"You don't have to do that. It didn't cost me a thing. Opal's boyfriend is part owner of the Chargers." Pearl looked around for Paige and Amber, who had conveniently disappeared, leaving her alone with the very man who seemed to dominate her thoughts lately.

"I should've asked you this earlier. Whose side are you on?" Pearl asked. "Chicago or Detroit?"

"For the record, I'm a Detroit Chargers fan."

"Good answer," Paige responded from behind them. "We're about to grab something to eat. Why don't you join us, Pastor?"

"You're sure?"

"What are you doing?" Pearl whispered to her cousin between stiff lips.

"Just being friendly."

She sent her cousin a sharp glare, sparking laughter from Amber.

Pearl managed to keep her expression blank while dining with Wade. She was acutely aware of Amber and Paige watching their exchanges. She was determined not to give them any insight into her feelings where this man was concerned.

Wade insisted on paying for dinner. "It's the

least I can do," he said. "I really appreciate the chance to watch the game with all of you."

"Being down where all the action is doesn't hurt," Amber stated.

Pearl sent her a sharp look.

Half an hour before the game was scheduled to begin, they left the restaurant and walked down to their seats.

"You look excited," Wade said.

"I am." She smiled. "I love basketball."

Her attention turned to the game when the announcer started talking.

It wasn't long before Pearl was on her feet, yelling, "That was an offensive foul, ref."

Turning toward Wade, she asked him, "Did you just see that?"

He nodded and said, "I wasn't aware that you knew so much about the game. Do you play?"

"No. I just enjoy watching." Her eyes darted back to the court. "C'mon, Lyman," she yelled. "Two points."

When he missed the basket, Pearl groaned. "That was a brick. Man, our shooting sucks tonight."

She glanced over at Wade, who sat there quietly. "Are you having a good time?"

"The best," he replied with a smile, his eyes never leaving her.

"You have a beautiful smile," Pearl blurted. "You really should show it more often."

"You have no problem speaking your mind. Do you?"

"Not at all. Life's way too short to play games. I don't know about you, Wade, but I intend to make the best of mine."

"I like your attitude."

"That's all?" Pearl asked with a smile. "After all this time, all I get is you like *my attitude?*"

He couldn't help but laugh. "Pearl, I like you. Every inch of you."

"Same here."

After her confession, Pearl returned her focus to the basketball game. It was almost over.

She stole a peek at Wade and smiled.

Wade had never met a woman as passionate about basketball as Pearl.

The Chargers tied the score with twenty seconds left in the game and called a time-out. Pearl and Paige both were yelling for their team.

"We need a Hail Mary," Paige stated.

"We need to get the ball back," Pearl responded with a grunt.

Amber leaned forward to say, "Pastor, I hope they haven't given you a headache like the one they've given me. I don't know why they have to do all that screaming. It's so unladylike."

"I'm fine," he replied. "They're sports fans. Just like the thousands sitting all around us."

"Maybe it's because I'm sitting beside them, but they sound a whole lot louder than everybody else."

Wade noticed a young man come to their section. Without saying anything, he passed a note to Amber and walked away.

After reading it, Amber stood up. "I'll be back."

The crowd screamed when the game resumed. As if they'd heard Pearl, the Chargers stole the ball, came down court and scored, sending Pearl and Paige into a frenzy. He chuckled, watching how animated they'd become, jumping up and down, flailing their arms and laughing.

Pearl stopped long enough to ask, "Why are you just sitting there? We just won the game." She reached down, taking him by the hand. "C'mon, get up and act like you're happy the Chargers won."

Wade loved the freedom Pearl exhibited and

wondered what life must be like for her. He'd never been the type of person to just let go like that.

Pearl glanced around. "Where's Amber?"

Her cousin's eyes searched the surrounding area, then she pointed. "She's over there talking to Dashuan," Paige responded.

"He sent someone over here with a message earlier," Wade told them.

Pearl frowned. "Amber should've just ignored him." She sat down in disgust.

"Are you okay?" Wade asked Pearl after a moment. He could tell from her expression that she was upset.

"I just don't like that guy. He's bad news and I don't want him anywhere near my sister."

Lately Dashuan Kennedy had been in the news quite a bit. Wade knew of his drug problem, his run-ins with teammates and his quick temper.

He didn't really know Amber well at all but Wade prayed she would be wise and listen to her sister and Paige. From what he'd seen of D'marcus Armstrong and Luther Biggens, they would see that no harm came to Amber.

"Your sister will be fine. She's just talking to the guy."

"I don't want her even doing that. Wade, you don't know my little sister. She's a big flirt but she doesn't deserve to be hurt. I'm telling you, Dashuan Kennedy is nothing but bad news."

"All you can really do is pray for her. She's going to do whatever she wants. She's a grown woman."

"Wade, I know you're right. It's just that with my sisters…we're all we got. We have to look out for one another."

Her words brought back a tragic memory that stabbed at his heart, causing a flash of pain.

"Wade, you okay?"

He nodded. Rising to his feet, Wade said, "Thank you again for the ticket. I really enjoyed myself."

"I'm glad you came." Pearl broke into a smile. "I hope we didn't embarrass you by all of our cheering and carrying on."

Wade laughed. "You didn't," he assured her.

"Think you'll come back to another game? We get tickets all the time. I'm sure I can get one for you."

He nodded. "And I'm clear that it's not a date."

Laughing, Pearl stood up. "I guess we're going to head out, too."

Paige followed them as they walked toward the nearest exit door.

"I'm going to meet up with Lyman," Paige announced. "I'll meet you at the car."

"Make sure Amber is with you," Pearl instructed. "She came with us and she's leaving with us."

She was fiercely protective of her sister, Wade noted. He admired that quality in Pearl although he hated the fact that it was something he sorely lacked all those years ago. He never should have allowed his brother to join the Chicago Kings.

Wade forced his mind back to the present, forcing the bile of regret back down his throat.

Pearl had just gotten into her apartment when the telephone rang. It was Wade.

"I wanted to make sure you and Paige made it home safely. I also wanted to say thanks once again. I really enjoyed myself tonight."

"So did I." Pearl couldn't help but smile.

"I know it's late but I felt like I should call."

"Not a problem. I planned on staying up to start on James Patterson's new novel as soon as I get into bed."

"I won't keep you, then. Have a good night, Pearl."

"Wade, do you have to go right now?" She wasn't ready to end their conversation.

"No, I was just going to find something to watch on television."

Closing her bedroom door, Pearl climbed into the middle of her bed. "I like talking to you," she told Wade. "Don't think I don't notice that I always seem to be the one sharing. Why don't you ever talk about yourself? Like when did you get the call to the ministry?"

"I realized I wanted to preach shortly before my nineteenth birthday. I was in my room one day in the middle of praying over a situation and then it just hit me. I knew what I was called to do."

"So you enrolled into the seminary?"

"Yes. Once I accepted the call on my heart, there was nothing else for me to do but to put it in action. That's what I did. The rest is history, I guess."

"Do you have any regrets?"

"About the ministry?"

"Yeah. Do you regret being a pastor?"

"No. Not at all. Every phase of my life, good and bad, has led me to this place. I am committed to my calling."

"I know that," Pearl murmured. "I can see that

for myself. I think it's admirable. I feel the same way when it comes to my singing."

"How's that going?"

"I'm still waiting for that one call—the one that will offer me a recording contract. I want my music to be heard all over the world. This is my ministry. I know it, Wade. I'm just waiting on God, but I'm ready."

"You are a gifted singer. I know the kids at church love you."

"I love them, too. They're faced with so much and they need positive role models. I love working with them."

"What happens when you strike it big and get everything you want? Are you planning on re-signing as youth-choir director?"

"I'm not just going to up and abandon my babies, Wade. I don't intend to resign, but until I actually get a contract, I don't know what will happen. I'm not doing anything without prayer, I'll tell you that."

"I hope I'm not being too personal, but why aren't you in a relationship with someone?"

"How do you know I'm not?" Pearl replied.

"Are you?"

"No. I'm waiting for God to send me my guy

on a lightning bolt. What about you? Why are you still single?"

"I believe you said it was because I was a stuffed shirt."

She laughed. "You've grown on me."

"I can say the same about you."

Pearl broke into a grin.

"You're smiling," Wade stated.

"How do you know?"

"I can feel it radiating through the phone."

"Wow, you sure know how to flatter a girl. More, more, more."

Pearl loved making Wade laugh. He was too young to be so serious all the time. Life was meant to be enjoyed.

She stifled a yawn and glanced over at the clock. She and Wade had been on the phone for a while.

"I'm sure you want to get your beauty rest. I'll let you go."

"Okay. Have a good night, Wade."

When she hung up, Pearl danced around the room singing, "He likes me…he likes me…."

Chapter 9

Pearl felt her eyes fill with water as she stared at the two manila envelopes with her name on them, having spotted them on her bed from the very first moment she walked into her room after work.

Rejection letters.

She knew that's what they were because she could feel her demo tapes inside and the labels were written in her familiar scrawl. How she dreaded them. Pearl could never fully prepare her heart for rejection.

Maybe I should go back to college and finish

up my degree. Lord knows I'm never going to be a singer. Pearl glanced up toward the heavens. "Okay, God, I get it. I'm never going to get a record deal," she whispered. "I give up."

As soon as the words slipped through her lips, Pearl knew she didn't really mean them. Singing was in her blood; she couldn't quit if she tried. Had anyone even bothered to listen to her songs?

She took off her uniform and changed into a pair of gray sweats. Then, she tossed the envelopes on her dresser and climbed into her bed.

Maybe I'll feel better after my nap, she decided. Pearl truly believed that life always looked better after a nice long nap.

She woke up forty-five minutes later when her sister came by for an unannounced visit.

"Pearl, what's wrong?" Amber asked as soon as she walked into the apartment. "You look terrible."

"Gee, thanks."

"You know what I mean. You look sad. The drapes are all shut. Did something happen?"

"I just received two rejection letters." Sighing in resignation, Pearl uttered, "I don't know, Amber. Maybe I should just give up this dream."

"Why are you saying that? Are those the only rejection letters you've received?"

Pearl nodded. "So far. The others will probably pour in over the next few days. Nobody wants my music."

"Don't you start being so negative. Pearl, you're always the one telling me to never give up on my dreams, that if God gives you a vision, he gives provision. You can't let this stop you."

Tossing her hair over her shoulders, Amber continued. "I have an idea. Let's go out for an evening of pampering. We'll have facials, manicures and pedicures. My treat."

"That's your answer to everything, isn't it?"

"Well, you think taking a nap is the answer to life's problems."

"I think we're both wrong."

Amber chuckled. "Or we could both be right. C'mon, Pearl. Go do something to that hair of yours and let's get out of here."

Puzzled, Pearl glanced in the mirror. "What's wrong with my hair?"

"It's all over your head. Pull it back or get a perm."

"This is my 'all is not well in my world' look. I think it fits my mood perfectly."

"It's your mood that we're trying to change," Amber reminded her. "Remember?"

"I'll tell you what will make me feel a whole lot better."

"What?"

"You staying away from Dashuan Kennedy."

Tossing her honey-blond tresses over her shoulders, Amber replied, "Pearl, don't start. I don't know why you don't like him. He's such a sweetheart."

"Do you ever watch the news?"

"I don't want to do this with you," Amber began. "Pearl, you're my sister and I love you dearly, but I really need you to back off."

"Amber, I don't want you to get hurt."

She quickly waved aside Pearl's concern. "I'm not. I'm just hanging out with Dashuan. I want to get to know him better. If he's as much of a bad boy as everybody is making him out to be, I'll see it for myself."

"You can read the newspaper for that, Amber," responded Pearl. "Why put yourself through the drama?"

"I like him."

"You're just in lust," Pearl responded sharply. "That's all that is, Amber."

"How would you know, Miss 'I'm Saving Myself for Marriage'?"

Pearl met her sister's gaze straight on. "You should be doing the same thing, little sister."

"Save the sermon for Sunday. Let's go pamper ourselves, Pearl. You deserve it and so do I."

"You're just determined to be hardheaded," Pearl complained.

Looping her arm through her sister's, Amber responded, "I know. I love you, too."

"Pastor called," Paige announced as soon as Pearl walked through the front door later that evening. "He wants you to call him back."

Hanging up her coat in the hall closet, Pearl inquired, "Did he say what he wanted?"

"Nope. Just that he needed you to call him back as soon as possible."

"Why are you looking at me like that?"

"Looks like you and Pastor must be getting pretty close."

"You're so far off the mark," Pearl uttered. "Anyway I'll give him a call tomorrow. I've just had a calming green-tea facial, been wrapped in seaweed, had a massage, a manicure and pedicure. All of which did nothing to make me feel much better. Today's not been real kind to me and I just don't feel like talking to anyone, including Wade."

"You received a rejection letter today."

"Two," Pearl corrected.

"Don't let it get you down."

"That's easy for you to say." Pearl sighed. "I just want this so badly." Her misery was so acute, it was physical pain. "I don't know if I can take any more rejection."

"If you want this as badly as you say you do, Pearl, you'll take these and more. Reaching your dreams isn't always an easy road to travel. But you can't give up."

She gave a tiny smile. "I hear you, Paige. Most days I believe what you're saying. Today…I don't know. Today is just a hard one."

"I'll make you some chamomile tea. Not even a fancy spa can relax you like a cup of hot tea."

Pearl walked over to her cousin and hugged her. "Thanks for the pep talk. I appreciate it."

"I believe in you, Pearl. Don't ever give up on your dreams."

Pearl had just gotten into her pajamas when Paige brought the cup of hot tea into her bedroom.

Pearl sipped it while reading a passage of scripture from her Bible. She leaned back against the stack of pillows and sighed. *Maybe I'm asking for too much,* she silently considered.

In her heart, Pearl didn't really believe that, but the way things were going she didn't know what to think.

"All I've ever wanted to do is sing. Lord, I know you gave me this voice for a reason. You gave me this dream for a reason. I'm waiting...."

Pearl yawned as she reread the passage of scripture. She could feel the tea working its magic through her system.

She closed her Bible, said a short prayer and crawled under the down comforter. Pearl closed her eyes and waited on sleep to overtake her. She was ready to get this day over with.

Maybe tomorrow would bring better news.

It was her prayer.

Pearl was still in a funky mood the next day when she woke up.

Wade called her shortly after 10:00 a.m. "I left a message for you to call me back last night," he told her as soon as she picked up the phone.

"Good morning to you, too."

"I apologize. Good morning, Pearl."

She wasn't in the mood for pleasantries, so she asked, "What did you need?"

"Are you available for lunch around noon?"

Pearl opened her mouth in surprise. Wade was asking her out on a date. A real date. Her heart sang with delight.

"Pearl," he prompted, "did you hear me?"

"Yeah. Sure."

"Perfect. Let's meet at Stonewood Grille."

She was still in shock. Pearl couldn't believe Wade had asked her out. Just the thought brought out a tiny smile. "I'll be there."

"I look forward to seeing you then."

They hung up.

It had been a struggle for Pearl to keep her feelings for Wade hidden, but now she didn't have to. They would be dating.

Humming, Pearl felt blissfully happy hours later as she strolled out of the apartment, on her way to meet Wade.

Chapter 10

Wade spied Pearl the moment she walked through the doors of Stonewood Grille. She saw him and waved, then made her way over to join him.

He stood up as she approached. "Thanks for meeting me, Pearl."

She sat down into the chair he'd pulled out for her. When he was seated, she said, "Wade, I have to admit that after our conversation the other night, I'm not totally surprised to be here. We've come a long way in a really short time."

He was confused by her statement. "I felt we needed to talk."

She was watching him intently. "You're right. We do."

Wade had a strong feeling that they weren't talking about the same thing. He decided to make his intentions clear. "Pearl, the reason I asked you here is to discuss the upcoming fashion show."

She hesitated, blinking with bafflement. "Excuse me?"

"I thought we could discuss the upcoming fashion show. I realize that you've worked hard on it, but—"

Pearl interrupted him, saying, "You invited me here to discuss the fashion show? Why didn't you just say that on the telephone?"

She looked irritated, so Wade said, "I'm not sure I understand why you're upset." Then it hit him. She thought this was a date.

Wade cleared his throat. "I'm sorry. I didn't mean to mislead you in any way."

"You really have a high opinion of yourself," she huffed. "Don't you? You just automatically assume this is about you." Pearl stopped her tirade when the waiter appeared.

Wade was grateful for the temporary reprieve, but he couldn't help feeling bad when he caught a glimpse of sadness in Pearl's eyes.

Wade hadn't meant to embarrass her or cause her pain.

She had never been more humiliated.

Lashing out to hide her embarrassment, she snapped, "Let's just get this over with. I assume there must be a problem with the fashion show." Her lips thinned with irritation. "What's wrong now?"

"I thought maybe we should discuss what's considered appropriate for the show since it is a church event."

"Are you kidding me?" she blurted. "I picked every single piece of clothing out myself."

"Pearl, I'm feeling this tension between us," Wade began. "Let's just forget the fashion show for the time being. I think we should talk about whatever is bothering you."

Pearl shot a commanding look at him. "I'm fine, Pastor."

"Are you sure?"

They stared at each other across a sudden ringing silence.

Pearl nodded. "Look, Pastor, I've been coordinating this fashion show for the past four years, and nobody has ever complained…except you." She hadn't meant to sound so snappish but she wasn't in a very good mood right now.

"The clothes arrived yesterday," Wade announced after a tense moment. "Why don't we go over to the church after lunch to make sure you have everything? This designer is a close friend of yours, I understand."

She nodded. "Sienne and I went to high school together."

When their food arrived, Pearl found she didn't have much of an appetite. She pushed her fish from side to side with her fork.

"Something wrong with your food?"

"No, it's fine."

He was still watching her, concern evident in his eyes.

"Wade, I'm sorry for snapping at you. It was wrong."

"You're obviously upset. I'm sorry if I—"

Pearl held up a hand to stop him. "It's nothing."

After lunch she followed Wade over to the church in her car, silently chiding herself for her behavior. She was so ashamed of acting like a spurned woman. But she'd had enough rejection already.

Barbara did a double take when she saw her walk in with Wade.

"Pearl, what are you doing here?" she asked. "I thought choir practice was held in the evenings."

Pearl refused to let Barbara upset her further.

Pearl released a deep cleansing breath, then explained, "I'm just here to check on the stuff for the fashion show."

She stood up. "I'll help you. There are some pretty pieces in there. I can't wait for Marnie to see them. They're just her style."

Barbara was still trying to bait her into an argument, but Pearl wasn't going to give her the satisfaction.

Wade unlocked the door across the hall from his office and pushed the door open.

Pearl walked in. "I need to do an inventory to make sure I have everything."

"Need any help?"

"I'm sure Sister Barbara has enough to do. I can manage."

"I was talking about me. I don't mind helping you for a little while."

Wade's offer surprised Pearl. "You want to help me with inventory? Why?"

"You have a lot of stuff here. I thought you could use the help."

"If you're sure you want to do this," Pearl stated with a slight shrug. "You don't have to, but I appreciate the help."

"Let's get started," he suggested.

Picking up a dress on a hanger, Pearl fingered the silken material.

Sienne was a gifted designer who'd worked for Jean Paul Gaultier until recently striking out with her own designs. Her clothing was beautiful and very well made. Pearl was truly happy for her friend's success, but she also felt a wave of disappointment.

Lord, what do I have to do? All I've ever wanted to do was sing for Your glory. Why can't I catch a break?

Wade held up a halter top. "This is what I'm talking about. It's a—"

"I know what it is," Pearl snapped. "And there's absolutely nothing wrong with it. I wear them all the time."

He shot her a penetrating look.

"I can't believe you're such a prude. Wade, it's a shirt."

"It's half a shirt the way I see it," he countered.

"It's all in how you wear it. You don't know a thing about fashion. I mean, look at you," she fussed. "You don't wear anything that isn't blue, black or brown. If you're feeling a little wild, you might throw in some gray. How boring is that,

Wade? This fashion show is about taking risks. You wouldn't know a thing about that."

Wade eyed her. "Pearl, I know something is going on with you. What's with the bad mood?" he asked. "Does this have to do with lunch?"

She sank down in a nearby chair. "No, Wade. This doesn't have anything to do with lunch. This has everything to do with the fact that you have absolutely no trust in me."

"What are you talking about?"

"I know what I'm doing, Wade!"

"I'm sure you know quite a bit about fashion. As you stated, I don't keep up with the latest trends, but I know my outdated fashion sense has nothing to do with the real reason you're upset. Pearl, will you please talk to me?"

"I'm starting to feel like I'm wasting my time with the music," she blurted. After a brief pause, she continued. "I got two rejection letters yesterday, Wade."

"I'm sorry," he offered. "But, Pearl, this is your dream. You can't walk away from this."

Her eyes filled with tears. "I don't want to quit, but how long can I keep dreaming?"

Wade checked his watch. "I have a meeting in

half an hour." He looked over at her. "Pearl, do you have any plans tonight?"

"More talk on the fashion show?"

He shook his head. "No, this is strictly social. I have tickets to see Tyler Perry's new play. Would you like to go with me?"

She considered his offer a moment. "Wade, you don't have to do this. I'm a big girl."

"This is not out of pity. Pearl, I'd really like you to go with me. It's been on my mind for a few days but I wasn't sure how you'd feel about it. I know I'm not your favorite person."

Disconcerted, she crossed her arms and looked away. "I wouldn't say that exactly."

"So what about it?"

"No talk about church, politics or fashion?" Pearl asked. "I want to go out and just have a good time."

"I promise none of those subjects will come up tonight."

She smiled. "What time should I meet you?"

"If you don't mind, I'd like to pick you up."

"Like a date?"

Wade laughed. "This *is* a date. Isn't it? It's been a while for me so I'm a little out of practice."

"We don't even want to go there," she replied

with a chuckle. Pearl gave Wade directions to her house.

"I'll pick you up at six," he told her. "The play starts at seven-thirty."

"See you then." Pearl picked up her purse. "Enjoy the rest of your day."

"You do the same," he responded. "And, Pearl, don't give up on your dreams. Seek God first and He will give you the desires of your heart according to His riches in glory. Stand on that promise."

"Thanks, Wade. I'll see you tonight."

Barbara was standing outside the office when she walked out. Pearl couldn't resist asking, "Oh, did you need to see Pastor?"

"No, I, uh, was just checking to see if you needed my help with anything."

"Thank you so much for offering, Sister Barbara, but I have everything under control."

Pearl wondered how much of their conversation the nosy secretary actually heard. She didn't want rumors flying all over the church about her and Wade.

"Pearl, dear, have you met my niece? She's a doctor, you know."

"I met her when I was at the hospital visiting with Paige."

"Why don't you invite my niece for lunch? I'd like for her to get to know you and your sisters."

"After the holidays, I'll try to plan something," Pearl stated.

"Don't forget now."

"I won't," Pearl responded. *Not that you'd ever let me,* she added silently. She wondered why Barbara wanted her to hook up with her niece.

"Have a blessed day," Barbara called out as Pearl made her way to the door.

"You, too," Pearl responded back. She was pretty sure that Barbara had overheard her conversation with Wade. Pearl suddenly understood what her mother meant when she used to say, "Keep your friends close and your enemies closer."

"Did I just hear her correctly, Pastor?" Barbara queried. "Did Pearl Lockhart say she was seeing you tonight?"

"That's correct." Wade waited for his secretary to comment further. He knew Barbara wouldn't leave it at that.

"She's a nice young lady…" Barbara glanced over her shoulder before adding in a loud whisper,

"A little on the wild side, if you ask me. Now, my Marnie…my niece is a little more conservative. That Pearl's been after you for a while. I knew it the Sunday she strutted in church with that short leather skirt on. Pastor, you did the right thing when you had her legs covered up. Now, my Marnie…she'd never do something like that. She's not aggressive like that and she definitely don't go around chasing down no man."

"Sister Barbara, thank you for your concern, but it's not necessary. I've spent time with Pearl and I consider her a friend." Wade hoped that his words would put an end to the conversation. He didn't want to be rude or hurt Barbara's feelings.

"Pastor, I'm not trying to tell you your business…but just be careful. 'A man that findeth a wife findeth a good thing.' That's what the Bible says. You know, Marnie is stopping by shortly. I'll make sure she comes to say hello to you."

Wade wasn't totally surprised that Marnie hadn't told her aunt about their conversation. He suspected there was much Barbara didn't know about her niece.

Checking his watch, Wade said, "I have a conference call scheduled to start shortly, so please hold all my calls."

Barbara strolled through the open door. "I'll make sure you're not disturbed, Pastor."

That includes Marnie, Wade added silently.

From what he knew of Barbara, he wouldn't be a bit surprised if she had Marnie sit and wait for the conference call to end. Wade checked his watch a second time.

He had enough time to call the florist and have some flowers delivered to Pearl. Wade hoped they would cheer her up. She looked so discouraged over the rejection letters.

Wade decided on a bouquet of exotic orchids and high-end chocolates. He was confident that she would be pleased by his selections.

"Pearl," he whispered, "I may not know fashion, but I do know flowers and chocolate."

Chapter 11

Their first date.

She and Wade were actually going on a real date. Pearl exhaled a long sigh of contentment. She couldn't wait for tonight. She had all kinds of hopes and expectations for the evening.

The doorbell sounded, breaking into her thoughts.

When she opened the door, she was met by a delivery man holding a gorgeous display of orchids and a gift-wrapped package.

"Miss Pearl Lockhart?"

Her body stiffened in shock. "These are for me?"

"Yes, ma'am."

She took the items from him and handed him a few dollars she had in her pocket.

Who had sent her flowers? They had to be from Paige or her sisters, she decided. Probably to cheer her up.

She gasped when she saw Wade had sent them. Pearl's eyes grew wet as she read the note of encouragement.

This is why I'm falling for him.

Shaking her head, Pearl whispered, "What am I doing? I can't think about Wade like this. He's the pastor of my church. He's stuffy. It just wouldn't work out. I don't see how it can."

She burst into laughter suddenly. "I can't believe I'm talking to myself. I'm losing my mind." Pearl knew she needed to stop making excuses for why a relationship between her and Wade wouldn't work. She cared for the man and was going on a date with him in a few hours.

Pearl glanced over at the flowers and the box of chocolates she'd unwrapped. Clearly, Wade felt something for her, as well. But even without all that, she could tell he was attracted to her. She only had to look into those expressive eyes of his.

Wade didn't wear his feelings on his sleeve the way she did, but Pearl could catch glimpses from time to time whenever he let his guard down, which wasn't often. There were times she felt as if Wade wanted to open up to her, but for whatever reason couldn't.

"There's nothing you can't share with me," she whispered. "I just need you to trust me. Trust me with your heart."

Pearl repeated the words. "Trust me…trust me with your heart." She ran into the library, straight to her keyboard.

She began playing, adding the lyrics to a song that had been floating around in her head for the past couple of days. "Trust me with your heart…."

She didn't stop until hours later when the phone rang. It was Paige calling to let her know that she'd arrived safely in Atlanta. She'd gone to spend a few days with Lyman.

"So what are you doing tonight besides watching the game?" Paige asked.

"I won't be home," Pearl responded. "I'm taping it to watch when I get back. I'm going to see Tyler Perry's new play."

"You going alone?"

"No," Pearl answered, "I'm going with Wade."

Paige gasped in surprise, prompting Pearl to burst into laughter.

"I told you," Paige managed to say, "you and Pastor have a thing for each other."

"It's *one* date."

"Pearl, be honest with me. You really like him. Don't you?"

"Yeah," she confessed. "It's something about him. Wade is nothing like any man I've ever dated." Pearl chuckled before adding, "That's a good thing."

"I think you guys make a cute couple. I hope it works out between you two."

"I'm not looking that far ahead," Pearl responded. "After tonight, Wade or I could decide we don't want anything other than friendship."

"Somehow, I seriously doubt that," Paige uttered. "You'd have to be blind not to see the chemistry between you and Pastor."

"Really? Is it that obvious?"

"Why do you think we've been trying to push you two together, Pearl?"

"Still, I'm not going to get my hopes up." Pearl glanced over at the clock. "Girl, I need to get off this phone. I need to get ready for my date."

"Have fun, Pearl. Call me tomorrow and give me all the details."

Two hours later, Wade rang the doorbell, exactly on time.

"You look beautiful," he said when she let him in.

"You don't look too shabby, either." Pearl pointed to the multicolored sweater he wore. "I can't believe you're wearing something other than black, blue or brown." Her mouth broadened in approval. "I'm proud of you."

Pearl reluctantly tore her eyes away his muscular body. She didn't want Wade to catch her staring so hungrily at him.

He moved about the living room, looked at the various photographs strewn about.

"Are these your parents?" Wade inquired.

"Yeah. They took that picture on their fifth wedding anniversary. I've always loved that picture. The way they're looking at each other—that's what I want. When a man looks at me that way, I'll know he's the one."

"What do you suppose he's thinking?"

"The man I'm destined to spend the rest of my life with…he'll know."

His gaze was as soft as a caress. "You and your sisters are very close," Wade observed aloud.

"All you ever really have is family," she murmured in response.

Wade was silent.

"Hey, you still with me?" Pearl prompted.

He glanced over at her and smiled, but she didn't miss the troubled expression that was on his face just seconds earlier. "We should get going. Are you ready to leave?"

Pearl nodded. "I just need to get my coat. I have to tell you I'm really looking forward to seeing this play. I've heard some wonderful reviews."

When they stepped onto the street, Wade reached over and took Pearl by the hand.

"I don't want you to slip and fall," he explained. "There was a light snowfall—enough for it to ice over."

"You just wanted to hold my hand. Admit it." The idea sent Pearl's spirits soaring.

Wade laughed. "Get in the car."

Throughout the play, something kept pulling Wade's attention to Pearl.

He couldn't keep from peering at her during the play. He reveled in her nearness. His body ached for her but he vowed to keep his desires under control. He had to practice what he preached no matter how much she tempted him.

It was easier to maintain his beliefs when he wasn't seeing anyone, but with a woman as beautiful and as fine as Pearl, it was going to be a struggle. Wade felt heat radiating from his loins and shifted in his chair.

"God give me strength," he prayed.

Pearl leaned over and whispered, "Did you say something?"

He couldn't miss the soft floral scent as she pressed closer. "No. Just enjoying the play."

She gave him one of her winning smiles before returning her attention to the stage.

At the end of the play, Wade stated, "Madea is an interesting character."

"I love her." Pearl wrapped her fuchsia-and-teal-colored scarf around her neck. "She loves her family. We have a couple of Madeas in my family. I think you met one of them—Aunt Becca."

He remembered Becca Lockhart clearly. "She was the one who kept calling me Wayne."

Pearl laughed. "Aunt Becca's no joke though. She has no problem using the gun she carries in that purse. Even the gangbangers don't mess with her."

Wade didn't comment. He sat there enjoying Pearl's closeness. Deep down, he was at war. His mind told him to resist Pearl, but his body refused. The web of attraction building between them could no longer be ignored.

"You're getting quiet on me again," Pearl said, "Is something wrong?"

"No. I was just thinking about something."

"Do you want to talk about it?"

"It's not important."

She didn't comment further. They followed the crowd through the exit doors.

Wade drove Pearl back to the apartment and parked the car. They sat inside, talking.

"I had a good time, Wade. Thanks for taking me to the play."

"The pleasure was all mine." He paused for a moment before saying, "Pearl, like I told you earlier, it's been a while since I've been involved with anyone. I'm not into casual relationships. I want you to know that."

"Neither am I," Pearl responded.

"I am looking for a woman I can settle down with," Wade announced. "While I'm not rushing it, I do want to get married one day and have a family."

She seemed to be peering at him intently. "I appreciate your honesty."

"I know that you want to sing professionally and I think you should go after your dreams."

"But…"

"But what?" Wade asked.

"I thought there was a *but* coming." Grabbing her purse, Pearl stated, "Well, it's getting late. I'd better go inside." Pearl reached over, squeezing Wade's hand. "I really had a nice time with you tonight."

"I'd like to see you again, Pearl."

"I'd really like that, too." She shot him a megawatt smile that had him thinking all kinds of things.

Wade couldn't get those thoughts out of his mind, even after he'd gotten home.

He was slowly losing his perspective where she was concerned. The more he tried to fight his feelings for her, the more they seemed to intensify.

Tonight, he'd practically told her that he was looking to be in a serious relationship. Wade wouldn't be surprised if she never wanted to see him again. He'd probably scared her off.

He considered calling her and trying to explain,

but decided against it. At the rate he was going, Wade worried that he'd blurt out a proposal.

Wade had never felt so connected to anyone the way he did with Pearl. But why Pearl? They were as different as night and day, yet they shared so much in common. It made absolutely no sense to him, but Wade knew that he felt incomplete whenever they weren't together.

Wade felt happier than he'd been in a long time, but the fact that he and his mother weren't on speaking terms put a damper on that happiness. It was almost Thanksgiving—a time when families came together.

He often wondered how his mother survived the holidays. Wade knew she missed his dad and brother, but what about him? Did she miss him, too?

He felt the familiar urge to call her, but resisted. His mother hated him and Wade couldn't take the rejection anymore. Like his guilt, it was a wound that would never heal.

After Wade dropped her off, Pearl didn't go up to her apartment. Instead she drove over to Opal's.

Her sister was dressed for bed. "I'm sorry for coming over so late but I really need to talk to someone." The words just rushed out of Pearl's mouth.

She followed her sister into her family room and told her about her date.

"We have such a good time when we're together. I really like him, Opal. I'm just not sure we should be dating."

"Why not?"

"I don't think it's going to work out."

But it didn't change the fact that she was falling in love with Wade.

Pearl put a hand to her face. "Opal, what am I going to do? I'm not willing to give up my dream. Not even for Wade. I can't be June Cleaver. That's just not me."

"I've never known you to just walk away without a fight," Opal stated. "If you truly care for Wade, then you have to give the relationship a chance."

"And get my heart broken?"

"How can you be so sure that's the end result?"

Mixed feelings surged through Pearl. "Because I'm not cut out to be the first lady of a church. Opal, I'm a singer and if I get a recording contract, Wade is not going to be able to handle my long hours in studios, months on tour. He wants someone who's more of a home-body like him."

"Why don't you let Pastor make that decision? He knows better than anyone what type of woman he wants to spend his life with."

"I have to end it," Pearl decided. "Before either of us gets hurt."

Opal shook her head sadly. "So you're going to just give up without a fight? Just like that, huh?"

Shrugging, Pearl muttered, "I don't know what else to do."

"Yes, you do," Opal countered. "Follow your heart."

When her sister started yawning, Pearl's eyes darted to the clock on the wall. "It's late." She rose to her feet. "Go on back to bed. I'll give you a call in the morning."

"Think about what I've said, Pearl."

"I will," she promised.

Fifteen minutes later, Pearl was home in her apartment. She readied for bed, but she was still awake after an hour of soul-searching. She eventually gave up and climbed out of bed, leaving the room.

In the dimly lit apartment, Pearl slowly made her way to the library.

She turned on the lights and sat down at her keyboard. When she couldn't sleep, she always came here to play. Music always had a way of soothing her spirit.

Tears in her eyes, Pearl played until she couldn't control her sobbing. She mourned what could never be.

She and Wade had no chance of a future together.

Chapter 12

Wade tried to shake his thoughts of Pearl out of his head but was failing miserably. His growing feelings for her wouldn't go away.

I care for her.

Despite his feelings, Wade had some doubts. He believed Pearl had strong feelings for him, as well, but could a relationship between them really work?

She wanted a recording contract. He needed a woman by his side in leadership of Lakeview Baptist Church in addition to being his wife and one day mother of his children.

Could he fully support her dreams while he put his own on hold when it came to marriage and family? Wade didn't have the answer to that question.

Only time would tell.

But could they just go back to being Pastor and Youth-Choir Director after crossing that invisible line?

In Wade's heart, he wanted more from Pearl.

Much more.

He and Pearl would take it one day at a time. They would enjoy every single moment of the time they had together, instead of dwelling on the future. If they truly cared for one another, nothing was impossible.

Still, he couldn't forget the uneasy expression on Pearl's face the night before when he spoke of his intentions. Wade needed to be sure of how she felt about him. There was a lot they needed to sort out.

He picked up the phone and dialed her cell phone.

When he heard the call being transferred to voice mail, Wade hung up. He made a mental note to try calling her later in the day.

A few minutes later, he heard voices outside his office.

Wade got up to see what was going on. He hadn't expected anyone to be there since tomorrow was Thanksgiving. He discovered Pearl a few doors down with her models. She was running around with a clipboard in hand, checking on this and that, wearing the signature smile on her face that never dimmed.

Wade loved hearing her bubbly laugh and the way she interacted with the other members, young and old. She had a good heart and a very nurturing spirit.

She smiled when she saw him walking toward her.

"Barbara said it was okay for me to use the banquet room for practice this afternoon. We're not going to be here long, Pastor. I just wanted to do a quick run-through before the fashion show on Saturday."

"No problem." Wade resisted the urge to stay and linger around her. He didn't want to create any speculation surrounding his relationship with Pearl. When the time was right, they would let everyone know.

Reluctantly, he returned to his office. But he was so distracted he couldn't get any work done.

Pearl suddenly appeared in the doorway. "Just wanted to let you know that we're leaving."

"Do you have a minute?"

"Sure." She walked into the office and sat down in one of the visitor chairs facing him, her thin fingers tensed in her lap.

"Are you busy tonight?"

"Wade, I think we need to talk."

There was a pensive shimmer in the shadow of Pearl's eyes, prompting him to inquire, "About what?"

"What's going on between us? I mean, what are we doing?"

His smile was genuine. "We're dating."

"I guess the more appropriate question is why are we dating?"

Her question set alarm bells ringing. Wade began wondering if he'd misread her actions. "I assumed we were attracted to one another."

"We are," Pearl confirmed. "I'm very attracted to you, Wade. I just worry that we're not headed in the same direction. You know how much I love singing. That's what I want to do. I want a record deal. I know that you want someone who will be the first lady of Lakeview. I'm not sure I'd qualify."

"Pearl, we have no way of knowing what the future holds. Let's just take this time to get to know each other. As I stated the other night, I'm not in a hurry to get married. I have some things in my own life that have to be worked out."

Frowning, she asked, "You don't have a wife hidden off somewhere, do you?"

"No. Nothing like that."

"I don't want to hurt you or be hurt."

"I'd never deliberately hurt you, Pearl. We'll take it one day at a time."

Pearl wavered. She stirred uneasily in the chair.

"I care a great deal about you," Wade stated. "I really want to explore a relationship with you."

"I want the same thing. Really, I do."

"You've asked me to trust you…well, I need you to trust me in this."

"I can do that."

Wade stood up. "I'm done here." He looked over at Pearl asking, "Have you eaten?"

"Nope. I'm starved. Didn't have breakfast this morning."

"Have lunch with me?"

Pearl seemed more like herself—more relaxed. "Can I pick the place?"

He nodded. "Sure."

"I'm driving," she told him when they walked out of the building. "We'll come back here for your car."

"Hot dogs?" Wade inquired when Pearl parked in the parking lot of Charlie's Coney Dog Empire. "You want a hot dog?"

"Coney dog," Pearl corrected. "You've got to try a Coney dog, Wade. This is probably my favorite food.

"You work at one of the most expensive restaurants in Detroit and this is what you like to eat?"

"Just wait until you taste one," Pearl responded.

Wade followed her into the restaurant and up to the counter. Turning to him, she asked, "Do you trust me?"

His arms encircled her. "Yes."

She ordered, "Four with everything. Grill the onions please."

They sat down on a couple of empty stools at the counter.

"Best seats in the house," Pearl explained with a chuckle.

"If you're ever in Chicago, you should try our hot dogs."

"What's so special about them?"

Wade grinned. "They're delicious."

"What's on a Chicago hot dog? Mustard and ketchup?"

"No ketchup," Wade responded. "Our buns

aren't plain like these—our hot dogs are beef and served on poppy-seed buns. We top them with mustard, onions, a pickle spear, tomato slices and you can't forget the celery salt."

"Celery salt? Sounds interesting, I'll admit. I'll have to try one."

Their orders were placed in front of them.

Pearl took a bite of her Coney dog after Wade blessed the food. "I don't think your Chicago dogs will come anywhere close to these."

Wade wiped his mouth with his napkin. "This really isn't bad." He took another bite.

"I told you that you'd like them. They're addictive. I have to have a Coney dog at least once a week. Paige calls them heart attacks on a bun." She chuckled. "But they're so worth the risk as far as I'm concerned.

"Do you miss Chicago?" Pearl asked between bites.

Wade shook his head. "Not really. I liked Gary much better, to tell the truth. And I love Detroit. At least as much of it as I've seen."

"Wade, do you have plans for Thanksgiving?"

He shook his head. "I'll probably go by Uncle Harold's house."

"Why don't you consider having dinner with

my family? We really have a good time when we get together. You saw us at the reunion."

"Is your aunt Becca coming?"

Pearl nodded. "She'll be there."

He laughed. "What will you tell your family if I show up with you?"

"Well, if we're going to be dating, there's no reason to keep it a secret. We might as well make the announcement over dinner. Goes great with turkey, don't you think?"

He cracked up with laughter. "I don't know what I'm going to do with you."

"I have a few ideas but you'll have to wait until we're married." Pearl glanced over at him. "I'm not trying to rush things, just so you know."

"Relax," Wade advised. "I can't believe I'm telling you, of all people, to relax."

"I can't, either." Pearl took another bite, chewing slowly.

"We're still on for tonight, right? Say around five?"

She nodded. "I enjoy spending time with you."

Wade reached over and cupped her face in his hand, holding it gently. "I feel the same way."

"So what do you have planned for tonight?"

He gave a slight shrug. "I thought we could take in a movie, but I'm open to suggestions."

"A movie sounds good," Pearl responded. "We can even rent one and watch it at my apartment."

"Will Paige mind my being there?"

"She's in Atlanta. She'll be home later tonight."

When they finished their lunch, Pearl drove Wade back to the church.

He leaned toward her, his lips brushed against hers. "Thanks for lunch. I'll see you in a few hours."

"Enjoy the rest of your day."

His eyes met her gaze for a moment, then his mouth covered hers hungrily.

Wade pulled away, his calm shattered.

"Bring those sexy lips of yours for tonight when we're alone," Pearl said. Flashing him a smile, she added, "I'll be sure to put on plenty of lip balm. You're a great kisser."

Shaking his head, Wade uttered, "What am I going to do with you?"

"If I told you, you'd have to marry me."

Pearl changed her outfit five times. She eyed her reflection in the mirror, frowning. "I don't want to wear this. It's too sexy. I don't want to start fires I can't put out."

By the time Wade arrived, she had settled on a simple red sweater and black jeans.

He took her by the hand as they headed into the living room.

"Worried about icy sidewalks again?" Pearl teased.

"No, this time I just wanted to touch you."

Pearl sat down on the sofa, smiling from ear to ear. When he joined her, she said, "I'm not going to keep teasing you like this."

"It's fine. I can take it."

"Were you able to rent the movies I suggested?"

Wade burst into a short laugh. "You didn't make a suggestion. You *told* me what you wanted to see."

"You wanted to see them, too." Her voice died as she moved toward him, impelled involuntarily by her own emotions.

Gathering her into his arms, Wade held her snugly. "This feels so right to me," he whispered.

Pearl buried her face against his throat.

"What's that smile for?" Wade asked.

"I'm really enjoying myself," she confessed.

"You sound as if you're surprised."

Pearl pulled away from him when she sat up. "Not really. Okay, I was a little worried that we might run out of things to talk about. C'mon, Wade, admit it. You felt the same way."

Wade laughed. "I must admit that I was a bit concerned initially."

"We're quite a pair, huh?" Pearl rose to her feet. "Would you like something to drink?"

"Just some water. Thanks."

Pearl disappeared off to the kitchen and returned a few minutes later with two bottles of water. She handed one to Wade, who smiled in gratitude.

His smile stirred something within her. Pearl unscrewed the top of her water and took a quick sip. "I don't know about you, Wade, but I'm still trying to get used to the idea of us dating. I never thought in a million years that the two of us would be out somewhere having dinner. There was a time I wasn't sure we could have a civil conversation."

"I know what you mean."

She eyed him. "Why? Did you think you were too good for me?"

Wade shook his head.

"Well, I thought I was too good for you," Pearl confessed. "As far as I was concerned you were nothing but doom and gloom. But the more I get to know you, that's not you at all."

"I thought you were a wild party girl."

Pearl eyed him in disbelief before bursting into laughter. "Naaah. You couldn't have thought that. Me?"

"I did. And I was so wrong."

"Well, I'm certainly glad you've come to your senses." Pearl picked up one of the movies and said, "Let's watch this one first."

Wade started the DVD, then returned to his position on the sofa, saying, "I've heard pretty good reviews about this film."

The mere touch of Wade's hand against her own sent a warming flush through her. She struggled to keep her mind on what he was saying. "I'm not sure Denzel can make a bad movie. He's a phenomenal actor."

Wade agreed with her. "I hope they don't use a lot of profanity in this film. Or graphic sex."

"I'm with you on that," Pearl uttered. "I don't need any more temptation."

He glanced over at her.

"What?" Pearl questioned. "I'm just being honest. I'm human and I'm not without my feelings. Wade, you're sexy. I can't lie about that."

He broke into a big grin.

"Don't I turn you on?"

Pearl could see that her inquiry caught Wade by surprise. "You don't have to answer that. I can see it all over your face."

Wade was extremely conscious of where Pearl's flesh touched him. He could barely keep his attention on the movie and was glad when it ended and Pearl gave him a tour of the library.

"This is the place where I get most of my inspiration," she said. "I love books and I love music. In this room, I have the best of both worlds."

Wade picked up some sheet music. "Are you working on a new song?"

Pearl nodded. "I've been working on this one for the past couple of weeks."

"Would you sing it for me?"

"Really?"

"I'd very much like to hear it."

She sat down at the keyboard and began playing.

"You want me to trust that you're working it out for meee…" Pearl sang, her fingers dancing over the keys. "It's so hard sometimes to break from the past…."

"You have such a beautiful voice," Wade complimented when she finished. "I love listening to you sing."

Her gaze met Wade's. "Thank you, but I think you're just being nice."

"Honey, I love the song," he told her.

"Really?"

"I could feel the passion emanating from your voice. I felt like I was listening to a private conversation with God."

"That's it exactly. I was singing it earlier and Paige heard it. She said the same thing."

"Pearl, I'm very proud of you and if this one song doesn't land you a record deal, I think you should put the CD out yourself."

"You really believe in me? Wade, you've said a couple of times that you don't really like my type of music."

"I won't lie to you," Wade replied. "I'm not a fan of a lot of the contemporary songs I hear, but, Pearl, you were right about one thing. The world needs more songs like this. I can't put into words how much this song just ministered to me."

"You're so good for my ego."

Wade wrapped his arms around her. "I'm not just saying it to make you feel good. I'm sure you know me better than that."

"Yeah," she agreed. "You have no problem letting me know how you feel about stuff."

"I could say the same thing about you. You're honest and I like that about you."

He closed the gap between them and kissed her.

Chapter 13

The impulse to pull Pearl closer to him, take the kissing a step further, was weakened by the truth that he was a man of God and therefore had no choice but to lead his life according to the Bible.

Wade pulled away from Pearl. "We have to stop."

"I know...but I don't want to," she moaned.

"Pearl...the things that you do to me. The way you make me feel..." Wade shook his head. "I need to get out of here."

"I don't want you to leave, but I understand. If you stay, things might get out of control."

He nodded. "I'm flesh and bone."

"Don't I know it," Pearl uttered. "My flesh is screaming right now."

"Will I see you tomorrow?"

Looking up at him, Pearl answered, "You can see me anytime you want. We're laying the foundation for a relationship, aren't we?"

"I think this goes beyond that, Pearl. My feelings for you are very strong. As you can see I'm having a hard time keeping them under control."

She kissed him lightly on the lips. "That's nothing but lust. I know because I feel it, too."

It took all of Wade's willpower to walk out the door. He had to walk fast before he changed his mind and gave into the passion that had been building for days.

Pearl stood with her back against the door. "Have mercy," she whispered.

She slowly made her way to the sofa and dropped down, unsure her legs would hold her any longer.

The man was the pastor of her church. She had to keep reminding herself of that fact.

He was still a man.

Why does he have to be so fine? she wondered.

Wade had no idea how sexy he was. He had no idea how his nearness affected her.

Pearl was still sitting in the same spot when Paige arrived home a little over an hour later.

"Hey, you," Pearl muttered. "How did you enjoy Atlanta?"

"I had a good time. Lyman and I didn't get to spend a whole lot of time together, though." Paige set her overnight bag on the floor beside the sofa. "Did you get a chance to see the game?"

Nodding, Pearl said, "I'm so glad they won."

Paige eased down on the arm of the chair. "So tell me, how did your date with Pastor go?"

"Well," Pearl responded, "as a matter of fact, Wade just left here not too long ago."

"What happened?"

"Nothing." After a brief pause, Pearl said, "Things just got a little hot and heavy tonight. I had to remind myself that I vowed to wait until marriage. And Wade's a preacher who has to lead by example."

Paige grinned. "Are you rethinking your decision to practice celibacy?"

Shaking her head, Pearl answered, "I'm just hoping for a short courtship." Rising to her feet, she said, "I'm kidding."

"Liar. Who do you think you're fooling? You want that man and in more ways than one."

"I want to do this the right way. I'm not a virgin—been there and done that, but I regret giving myself to the wrong man. I'd like to have something special for my husband on our wedding night other than something I bought from a store."

"I guess I'm not there yet," Paige confessed. "I don't think I could do it. Besides, I want to know what I'm getting."

"I have faith. God is going to send the right man for me. He'll be a perfect man in every way."

"You just want that man to be Wade, right?"

Pearl eyed her cousin. "I believe that man *is* Wade. Paige, when he holds me in his arms, it feels like I've come home. It feels right."

The telephone rang, interrupting her admission. "Hello."

"Where have you been?" Ruby questioned. "I've been calling all evening. Why didn't you answer your cell phone?"

"I had something to do," Pearl stated. She didn't mention that she was home with Wade. There would be too many questions if she did.

But Ruby wasn't satisfied.

"So where were you earlier? It's not like you to not answer your cell. I called Milton's and they told me you weren't working tonight."

"I was with a friend."

Before Ruby could inquire whom she was with, Pearl changed the subject. "When was the last time you spoke with Luther?"

"We talked earlier today. Why?"

"Just thought I'd ask," Pearl murmured with a chuckle. She knew Ruby had feelings for Luther that went beyond friendship.

"He's coming to the house for Thanksgiving," Ruby said. "I went out and bought another folding table. Our family grows every year."

Pearl laughed. "That's not unusual."

"You know what I mean." Not missing a beat, she added, "Speaking of which, what time are you coming over tomorrow? I'm trying to make sure we have our schedules in sync. I want dinner to go well."

"It will, Ruby," Pearl assured her. "Stop worrying."

Ruby was going to drive all of them insane over Thanksgiving dinner.

Pearl didn't want to be too hard on her oldest

sister. Holidays had always been special in their family. Ruby felt that it was her duty to keep up the tradition. Even if it made them crazy.

"I have deep feelings for Pearl," Wade said into the telephone. "Uncle Harold, I've never felt this way about anybody."

"She seems like a nice girl."

"She is," Wade agreed. "And she doesn't take any stuff from me. Pearl has no problem putting me in check. I love that about her."

"I'm telling you now that Ivy's going to be disappointed you won't be joining us for Thanksgiving. You know you're like one of our own. My wife likes to have her children home for the holidays."

"If you don't have any plans tomorrow morning, why don't you let me take you and Aunt Ivy to breakfast? We can go to the restaurant she likes so much on Grand River."

"Iridescence." Harold laughed. "You trying to butter her up?"

Grinning, Wade asked, "Think it'll work?"

"You have about a fifty percent chance. Bring her some flowers—that'll better your chances."

Wade arranged a time to meet at the restaurant.

"Have you tried to call your mother? You should wish her a happy Thanksgiving."

"No. Uncle Harold, she doesn't want to hear from me. I get it."

"I don't know about that, Wade. She sounded different the last time I spoke to her."

"I can't call her, Uncle Harold."

"Why not, son?"

"How can I expect her to forgive me if I can't forgive myself?"

Chapter 14

"I can't wait to see your sisters' faces when you tell them about you and Pastor."

Pearl looked up from the white chocolate she was melting for her Thanksgiving bread pudding. "Opal pretty much knows about us, but Ruby and Amber don't. I don't think it's going to be that much of a surprise, really."

"They all know that you and Wade are attracted to each other, but they have no clue that you've been spending time together for weeks. The only reason I know is because I live with you. You've been trying to be slick about it, but I know you've been seeing Wade. Girl, I'm not stupid."

"We just didn't want to say anything to anybody until we were sure of what was going on between us. We needed to define our relationship."

"Have you?"

Pearl nodded. "We're together. We're a couple, Paige. We care deeply for each other."

Her cousin embraced her. "I'm so happy for you. I have Lyman, Opal has D'marcus and now you have Wade. It's about time we all grabbed some good men. I'm telling you—it's our season for love."

Pearl laughed. "Lyman has turned you into a true romantic. I'm the one who always used to read romance novels and dreamed of finding my Prince Charming."

"There's nothing wrong with happily ever after. I never thought I'd love anyone as much as I love Lyman. Pearl, we've become so close this past year that I really think he's going to propose soon." Paige bent down to peek into the oven, checking on her cake.

"Really?"

She nodded. "I can feel it. Lyman is going to ask me to marry him soon."

"Maybe it'll be your Christmas present," Pearl suggested.

"That would make it the best Christmas ever. But I'm not going to get my hopes up. I don't want to be disappointed."

Pearl poured the melted white chocolate into a mixture of egg yolks, sugar and whipping cream. Stirring, she said, "This is almost ready. Have you sliced up the French bread yet?"

Paige nodded. "It's over there. I've already put it in the pan. I can't wait to sample the bread pudding when it's done."

"I had to call Aunt Becca to get the recipe. You know she doesn't measure a thing so I hope this comes out okay."

Paige laughed. "Now you're beginning to sound like Opal."

Shaking her head in disbelief, Paige added, "I still can't believe that the holidays are already here. Before you know it Christmas will have come and gone."

"What's that Aunt Becca always says? 'Time waits for no one.'"

Pearl couldn't help but smile at the thought that flitted through her mind.

This was finally her time.

* * *

"You look happy, Wade," Ivy observed aloud. "Tell me. Does this have anything to do with the young lady who sang at Cassie's wedding? Harold told me that she stole you away from us for dinner tonight."

She glanced around the restaurant. "This is your way of asking my forgiveness, I'm assuming." Ivy picked up the bouquet of flowers he'd given her. "Nice touch." Cutting her eyes at her husband, she added, "Very original. I guess you must really care for this young woman."

Wade broke into a smile. "Pearl and I have been seeing each other socially. We've become very close."

"Sounds to me like you're falling in love," Ivy stated.

Wade nodded. "I've always had a certain type of woman in my mind—the type that I thought I would end up marrying. On the outside, Pearl is nothing like her, but once you get to know her she's exactly the type of woman I want to share my life with."

"Have you told Pearl anything about Jeff or your mother?"

"No."

"Wade, she needs to know the man she's fallen in love with. Not just who you've become but who you were," Ivy advised. "You need to let Pearl see the real you, not just one part of who you are."

He wasn't sure he wanted Pearl to know about that part of his life, lest he lose her or her respect. "I'm not sure I can do that, Aunt Ivy."

"She's going to wonder about that look on your face whenever you're around her family or any family, Wade. Son, you can't hide forever."

"Ivy's right," Harold chimed in. "You need to finally confront your past. If you don't, you'll never really be free to move on."

"I've moved on," he countered.

"Not really," Ivy stated. "There's a big part of you still left in the past. Wade, if this woman cares for you, she *will* understand. Maybe if you talk about what happened, it'll help free you."

Wade realized he had a lot to consider before he and Pearl took their relationship further.

When he returned home later that morning, Wade thought back to his disturbing conversation with Harold and Ivy. How could he tell Pearl that he was responsible for his brother's death? That he'd been an active member of the Chicago Kings? She had no respect for gangbangers.

He was a man of God now. When he gave his life to Christ, his past was forgotten, so Wade saw no reason to bring it up to Pearl. But she wanted to know about his past. She'd already started asking questions.

Wade didn't want to lie to her. It wasn't a choice. But he didn't think Pearl would ever understand.

What was he thinking by accepting her invitation to Thanksgiving dinner with her family? It was an emotional holiday for Wade, which could lead to more questions—questions he wasn't ready to answer.

This was a mistake.

One that had to be rectified before it was too late. He called Pearl.

She had just taken her lemon pound cake out of the oven.

"I hope you'll bring a huge appetite today," Pearl said when she heard his voice. "We have tons of food."

"Pearl, I know this is really last minute, but I'm afraid I won't be able to come."

He didn't miss her quick intake of breath. "Why not?"

"It's just that I don't think I'm ready for all that. We've just started dating."

"All what?" Pearl questioned. "Wade, this is

just Thanksgiving dinner, for goodness' sake. I won't take it as a proposal of marriage if that's what you're thinking."

"I'm sorry but I can't make it," Wade responded. "Thanks for the invitation."

Pearl wasn't done. She was still demanding answers. "Wade, what's really going on with you? Why are you doing this now? Why won't you talk to me?"

"I just need some time, Pearl," he said with quiet emphasis. "This is moving a little too fast for me."

There was nothing but dead silence on the other end.

"Take all the time you need," Pearl replied, putting an end to the quiet. "Have a happy Thanksgiving, Wade. No, make that have a great life."

"Pearl—"

It was too late. She'd already hung up.

Pearl was hurt and probably angry with him, but there was nothing Wade could do about it. What could he really say to her?

It was best this way, he kept telling himself.

His heart was not convinced.

Wade had never felt as lonely as he did right now. It was as if a large chunk of him was missing.

I knew this relationship didn't have a chance. So why did I allow Wade to get so close to me?

Pearl hastily wiped away her tears when Paige walked into the kitchen.

"I thought I'd bring—" Her voice died as she noticed Pearl's expression. "You okay?"

"Yeah. I'm fine. Just trying to finish some things before we head over to Ruby's." After a brief pause, Pearl added, "Wade won't be joining us after all. He's decided it's too much for him."

"You're kidding, right?"

"I wish I was, but I'm not." Her voice broke. "He's not coming."

"Pearl, I'm so sorry."

Shrugging in mock nonchalance, she responded, "It's fine. Wade's nothing but a big chicken. He's afraid of committing to me and that's why he really backed out. It's his loss."

"I know it's breaking your heart, though."

"I'm hurt," Pearl confessed. "But I'll get past it. I should be focusing on my music anyway."

"I can't believe he'd do something like this to you." Paige shook her head in confusion. "You guys were getting so close."

"Let's change the subject," Pearl suggested. "I

don't want to dwell on Wade Kendrick another minute. He doesn't deserve it."

She pretended not to be affected by this turn of events, but Pearl found herself blinking back tears.

Paige stepped in her path, embracing her. "He'll come to his senses. Wade will be running back to you."

"I'm not so sure I want him back." She forced a laugh. "Not that I ever really had him in the first place."

Pearl made the decision that it was time to move forward with her life. Wade was now a part of her past.

"Anyway, happy Thanksgiving, Paige," she said as cheerfully as she could muster. "We've got a lot to be thankful for this year. I don't want to talk about Wade. It's over. I intend to focus on my future. And today I'm going to enjoy the holiday with my family and friends."

Paige nodded in agreement. "Ruby wants us at the house early," she announced.

Paige gave a slight shrug. "She wants to have dinner ready no later than four. You know your sister. Everything has to be perfect. I was getting

ready to put the broccoli-and-cheese casserole in
the oven but I'll just bake it over there."

The ringing telephone cut into their conversation.

"You think it might be Wade?" Paige asked.

Pearl glanced at the caller ID. "It's your sister,"
she announced, trying to hide the disappointment
in her voice. She'd hoped for a moment that Wade
had come to his senses. Apparently not.

It was truly over.

Chapter 15

"I thought Wade might be joining us today for dinner," Opal whispered when she managed to get Pearl alone. "You didn't ask him?"

"I invited him, but he won't be coming," Pearl answered succinctly.

"Why? Did he have other plans?"

"He's not coming, Opal. The end." Her voice was shakier than she would have liked.

"Doesn't sound like it."

"I don't want to talk about it right now," Pearl responded, her eyes narrowing. "Just drop it, Opal."

"Are you okay?"

A heaviness centered in her heart. "Having the time of my life."

Ruby interrupted them. "Let's get the table ready. I bought some new tablecloths. We'll put the floral ones on the smaller tables for the kids."

"I'll do the tables," Pearl volunteered. "You guys get started on something else."

"I can help you," Opal offered.

Eager for some time alone, she said, "I'd rather do it by myself. I'm sure there's plenty you can help with in the kitchen."

Ten minutes later, Pearl had the dining-room table set. Aching with an inner pain, she went to work on the children's table in the breakfast nook.

Amber came running into the kitchen. "Pearl, you've got a visitor."

She glanced over her shoulder, asking, "Who is it?"

"Come see for yourself."

"Why can't you tell me?"

Amber released a short sigh. "Pearl, would you please go out there and greet your visitor?"

Puzzled, Pearl left the kitchen. She couldn't come up with a single clue as to who her visitor was. She wasn't expecting anyone.

Especially Wade.

Pearl stared at him in shock. When she found her voice, she asked, "What are you doing here?"

"If I remember correctly, I was invited. By you."

"You also turned down the invitation," Pearl pointed out, keeping her voice low. "Or are you trying to make me believe I dreamed that part? Look, Wade, I don't know what game you're playing but—"

He held up a hand to silence her. "Pearl, I'm sorry about this morning. I—I was just— I can't really explain it, but all I know is that I love you and I want to be here with you today. Unless you'd like me to leave."

She resisted the urge to run into his arms. "I can't do this, Wade. I can't go back and forth. It's not something I do very well. I know that you keep so much of yourself private and I respect that, but if you want me to be a part of your life, you're going to have to remove this wall you've erected around you."

"I'm trying, honey. If you'd just bear with me…" Wade paused for a moment, then said, "I know what that look meant."

Pearl frowned. "What are you talking about?"

"Your parents' anniversary photo," Wade explained. "Your father was looking at your mother like that because he wanted her to *see* how her love affected him. He wanted her to be able to see a reflection of the love they shared. She was his soul mate, his best friend, the love of his life. She was his first love. Pearl, your mother was his only love."

Pearl gasped in surprise. "How did you know that? Did my sisters tell you?"

It was his turn to look surprised. "Tell me what? What are you talking about?"

"My mother was the only woman Daddy ever loved. They were childhood sweethearts. But only my family and close friends knew that. How did you find out?"

"Everything I just said describes the way I feel about you, Pearl. You told me that only one man would know that stuff—honey, that man is me."

In an unexpected move, Wade pulled Pearl into his arms, kissing her.

"Oh, my," someone behind them exclaimed.

Pearl stepped away from Wade to find Paige standing in the doorway grinning from ear to ear. She wasn't alone, however. Opal and Ruby were with her.

Clearing her throat, Ruby said, "I'm glad you could make it, Pastor. Happy Thanksgiving."

His arm still around Pearl, Wade smiled and responded, "Happy Thanksgiving to all of you."

Opal took Ruby by the arm. "We'll be in the kitchen," she announced. "Finishing up the cooking."

Paige gave Pearl a secretive smile before following her cousins. "I guess I'll join them in the kitchen."

"Alone at last," Wade murmured.

Pearl looked up at him. "So what does this all mean, really?"

"I want to be in your life and I want you in mine. I love you."

"I meant what I said, Wade. I can't have you coming in and out of my life. You either want to have a relationship with me or you don't. It's that simple."

"Understood," he murmured. "Pearl, I'm here because this is where I want to be. I mean it."

She broke into a smile. "In that case, welcome to the house where I grew up." Pearl gestured around. "I have so many happy memories here. I'm sure you feel the same way about the house you grew up in."

He gave a slight nod.

Pearl pulled him over to the mantel above the fireplace. She picked up one of the photographs. "This picture was taken the night of my singing debut."

"How old were you?"

"I was about six years old. That's when I realized I wanted to be a singer. It felt like coming home. I can't explain it any better than that. I just knew it was my calling."

"I understand exactly what you mean. That's exactly how I felt about preaching."

He looked at some of the other photos. "You look like both of your parents."

"Amber and I have more of my father's personality. Ruby and Opal are more like our mother." Pearl pointed to another photo. "This is the last family picture we took. Daddy died a week later."

Wade peered closer. "Is that you?"

"Yeah."

"You are a cutie," he murmured. "I like the hair."

Pearl laughed. "My rabbit ears."

Wade looked at all of the photographs on the mantel, committing to memory the relatives who were expected to join them today for dinner.

Luther arrived first, bringing in a spiral-sliced ham. "Happy Thanksgiving."

Pearl relieved him of his burden and carried it to the kitchen. Wade followed her.

The talking died down to a soft whisper when they walked into the kitchen.

"Why'd everybody get so quiet?" Pearl questioned.

Luther strolled into the kitchen behind them saying, "I figured I'd come rescue the good Pastor."

"I'm going to stay in here and help with the food. I'll be out shortly," Pearl stated. She accepted the kiss Wade placed on her lips.

When she turned around, all eyes were on her.

"Is there something you need to tell us?" Amber questioned.

Pearl pretended she had no idea what her sister was talking about. "I'm not following you."

"Are you dating Pastor?" Amber questioned. "I certainly hope you are after that kiss he just laid on you."

"That wasn't anything," Paige uttered. "You should've seen the one he laid on her earlier. I thought I was going to have to put out a fire in the living room."

Grinning, Pearl announced, "Wade and I are together."

Amber laid down the knife she'd been using to slice the cabbage. "When exactly did this happen? How come I'm just finding out?"

"The day they got into that heated debate at the family reunion," Paige responded. "We all saw it coming."

"What are you talking about? Wade and I didn't even like each other then. At least, I didn't like him."

Amber laughed. "The sparks were flying. You just didn't see them."

"He's a good man," Pearl murmured. "I never would've thought I'd be saying this in a million years, but I really believe he's the one."

Opal hugged her. "I'm so happy for you." Lowering her voice to a whisper, she added, "I'm really glad you followed your heart."

"Me, too," Pearl whispered back. "He makes me very happy."

"Did you get your sisters' approval?" Wade asked when she joined him in the living room.

Pearl looked up at him. "I don't need their approval. But, yes, they're happy about us."

"I'm glad."

"You weren't worried, were you?"

"Not really, but it's nice to know you have the support of family."

Pearl nodded in agreement. "You're right. One thing is for, sure we Lockhart sisters stick together."

"Noted."

She laughed. "I'm really happy you changed your mind about coming today. After our conversation last night, I didn't think we'd see each other again. I was even thinking about going to a different church."

"I overreacted. That's all."

Taking his hand in hers, Pearl said, "This is our first holiday together, you know."

"The first of many," Wade responded.

She placed a finger to his lips. "Let's just take it one holiday at a time."

"I love you, Pearl. I'm asking you to trust me. Honey, I won't do anything to hurt you. I want to be with you and I don't intend on going anywhere. You'll have to be the one to leave."

"Wade, I love you, too."

"Did I shock your family earlier when I kissed you?"

"You shocked all of us. I never expected you to show your emotions so publicly. This is a very different side of you I'm seeing."

"I did it because I wanted to prove to you how much you mean to me. I hurt you this morning and I wasn't sure you'd give me a chance to make it up to you."

"So you figured kissing me passionately in front of my family and friends would do it?"

"It worked, didn't it?"

"Naaah. Your showing up did it. The kiss was just the icing on the cake."

More of her relatives began arriving.

Pearl left Wade in the den with D'marcus and Luther while she helped her sisters with the final touches to dinner.

"Everything's ready," Pearl announced a few minutes later. "I don't know about you all but I'm starving."

Rising to his feet, Wade smiled in response. "I think you're always hungry."

Her hands on her hips, Pearl said, "You didn't just call me out like that?"

"Girl, everybody knows how much you like to eat," Amber teased.

Her other sisters got in on the light bantering. Laughing, Pearl glanced over at Wade, noting the suddenly somber expression on his face.

She eyed him. "Sweetheart, are you okay?"

For the past ten years, Thanksgiving depressed Wade. The holiday only caused him to mourn for all he'd lost. He'd felt this way during the years he lived with Uncle Harold and Aunt Ivy, but they had always been an extension of his family. They had always gone out of their way to make the day special for him, serving all of his favorite foods and watching his favorite movies.

It was still hard for him. Wade missed his family.

Jeff and his father were dead, but his mother was still very much alive. The fact that she still refused to have anything to do with him hurt him more than he'd admitted.

Wade had no idea his pain was evident on his face until Pearl checked to see if he was okay. She was still watching him and waiting for his answer.

"I'm fine."

He could tell by Pearl's look that she wasn't convinced.

"Where can I wash my hands?" he asked. He needed a moment alone.

"Right down this hall and it's the first room on the left."

He followed her directions to the bathroom.

When he returned, Pearl was waiting on him. "I hope you have an appetite. We have enough food to feed a small army."

Together they navigated into the dining room

where the others had gathered. Wade pulled out a chair for Pearl, then sat beside her.

"Pastor Wayne, what's going on between you and my niece?"

"Aunt Becca, his name is Wade," Pearl stated.

"That's what I said, child. Now mind your business. I was talking to Pastor Wayne. I want to know what his intentions are toward you."

Pearl opened her mouth to respond, but Wade reached over, taking her hand in his. "Honey, it's okay. I'll answer to whatever she calls me."

"Pastor, would you give the blessing please?" Ruby asked.

"Sure," Wade responded. "Let's bow our heads."

He prayed a short prayer of thanks.

"Amen," they all said in unison.

Pearl handed Wade a plate of hot yeast rolls. "Aunt Becca made these from scratch. I have to warn you—you can't eat just one."

"I'll try and restrain myself," he responded with a chuckle. "I intend to leave some room for dessert."

She watched him for a moment. Wade seemed fine on the surface, but Pearl couldn't shake the feeling that something was still bothering him.

What's really going on with you, Wade? she wondered in silence.

* * *

Wade's thoughts landed on his mother. He couldn't help but wonder how she was faring on this day. Holidays were hard for him, so Wade supposed they were the same for her.

He'd looked forward to spending Thanksgiving with Pearl, but seeing her with her family did exactly what he feared it would. It made missing his own family worse.

He could feel the heat of Pearl's penetrating gaze on him and glanced over at her. Wade gave her a tiny smile before returning his attention to his half-empty plate.

"I know you're going to eat more than that, aren't you?"

Wade reached for the macaroni and cheese, saying, "I'm just getting started." He then picked up the platter piled high with ham, placing a couple of thin slices on his plate.

While he ate, Wade listened to Pearl and her sisters bantering back and forth.

Amber took a sip of her iced tea before asking, "I think we've waited long enough. Pearl, are you and Pastor officially a couple now? Are you going to make the official announcement?"

Pearl wiped her mouth with her napkin. "I thought his being here was the announcement."

She glanced over at him. "But, yes, Wade and I are dating."

A round of applause rang out.

Pearl reached over, squeezing his hand.

When they settled back down, Opal said, "I guess the floor is open for announcements. I have one. D'marcus has asked me to marry him and I said yes."

Squeals of happiness sounded around the room as the sisters got up to hug and congratulate Opal and D'marcus.

"Welcome to the family," he heard Pearl say.

Pearl and her siblings returned to their seats while others murmured their congratulations to the couple.

Opal looked across the table at Wade, saying, "Pastor, we'd like you to perform the ceremony."

"I'd be honored," he responded.

Wade wasn't sure how much more of the loving family and group happiness he could take. He felt his chest tighten and his heart start to race.

Maybe this had been a bad idea, he thought to himself. Uncle Harold and Aunt Ivy were right. He was going to have to tell Pearl something and soon.

Feeling like it was getting hard for him to

breathe, Wade abruptly pushed away from the table, excusing himself. "I need to get some air."

Pearl moved to stand but he told her, "Just give me a minute. I'll be right back. Finish your meal."

The animation left her face. "Wade…"

"I won't be long," he promised.

Before she could utter a word, Wade had left the dining room.

Chapter 16

"Is he okay?" Amber asked.

"Yeah," Pearl responded, trying to swallow the lump that lingered in her throat. "He's fine. Just needs some fresh air."

Deep down she knew it was something more. If only Wade would talk to her, maybe she could help him in some way.

She wanted answers and Pearl intended to get them today. She wiped her mouth with the corner of her napkin, then got up from the table. "I'll be right back. I'm going to check on Wade."

She followed him outside the house and into the winter chill. "Wait up."

Catching up to Wade, Pearl pleaded, "Please tell me what's going on with you. Why do you get this profoundly sad look on your face sometimes? And don't try to tell me that you don't because I'm not blind. I can see it all over your face. You have that same look right now. Sweetheart, what are you thinking about?"

He shook his head regretfully. "Being here, around your family like this, reminds me of how much I miss my own family."

"I can understand that. I know how much I miss my parents." Pearl reached over and took his hand. "Wade, you don't have to feel like you're alone. You have me."

"I know you mean well, Pearl, but it's not the same. It doesn't even come close."

"I'm not sure I understand."

Wade didn't respond.

"Talk to me, Wade. You know you can trust me."

After a moment, Wade responded, "I'm the reason my brother's dead."

Pearl eyed him. "Sweetheart, what are you talking about? How are you responsible?" She didn't believe for a minute that he had anything to do with his brother's death.

"I used to be in a gang, Pearl. I was a member of one of the oldest and largest gangs in Illinois. The Chicago Kings."

"You?" Pearl took a step backward, not believing what she'd been told. Wade involved in a gang. It was preposterous. "I don't believe it."

"It's true."

Shaking her head, Pearl uttered, "I don't understand, Wade. The man that I know you to be wouldn't be a part of something like that. The man you are—"

"Is a result of what happened back then," he finished for her. "I know how you feel about gangs, but back then it was a different time. Pearl, I was a different person ten years ago. Losing Jeff and my mother changed me for the better. I was on the wrong path."

She didn't say anything; she just stood there shaking her head in disbelief.

"You were a gangbanger? I just can't wrap my head around this."

Wade nodded. "It was my life at one time. After my dad died, things just didn't really make sense. I didn't care about anything. I went from being my father's son to being part of the Chicago Kings family."

"What about your mother? How did she feel about all this?"

"When Dad died, she started working more and more. When she found out I'd joined a gang, she was upset and she kept trying to get me to leave the Chicago Kings, but I didn't want that. They were my family. Mom made me promise that I'd never let Jeff become a part of that life. Back then, I didn't value anything. When my baby brother wanted to join us, I didn't have a problem with it. Me and my boys, we'd protect him. That was my attitude."

"How did your brother die, Wade?"

His eyes darkened with pain. "Jeff was killed in a drive-by shooting." A look of tired sadness passed over him. "That day has haunted me for the past ten years and it's not an easy thing for me to talk about, Pearl."

"Try. Wade, please tell me what happened."

"We had a beef with a rival gang. One of their boys was killed near our turf and they thought we did it."

"Did you?" Pearl held her breath while waiting for the answer. She didn't know how she'd react if Wade confessed to killing someone.

He shook his head. "We didn't have anything to do with that boy being killed. But that didn't matter. They came gunning for us anyway." Wade closed his eyes, reliving the pain of that memory. "That particular day, Jeff and I were out hanging with another member, T-Bone. I remember walking down the street talking and laughing one minute and then seeing Jeff on the ground covered in blood. I knew T-Bone had been hit, too, but he kept telling me to check on my brother. It wasn't until later that I found out he was paralyzed from the waist down. I guess I must have panicked and hid, leaving them…" Wade shook his head sadly. "The Kings wanted to avenge Jeff's death and T-Bone's shooting. We found one of their members and beat up on him. I'd always thought I could take a life until that night. I couldn't kill that boy and I wouldn't let my brothers shoot him. Not even for Jeff. I felt like a coward."

He sighed heavily, his voice filled with anguish. "The day my mother buried Jeff was the last day she spoke to me."

"No." Pearl placed a hand to her mouth.

He nodded. "I don't blame her. Pearl, my brother would still be alive if I'd made better choices. If I'd kept my word to my mother, I wouldn't have lost them both."

She could see the strain the years of torment had placed in his face.

"You've kept this bottled up all these years, haven't you?"

"I've told you more than I've ever told anyone, including Uncle Harold. I just couldn't talk about it. I can only imagine what you must think of me now that you know the truth."

Pearl kissed him. "Sweetheart, I still love you. Wade, you were a kid back then. Do you remember your sermon just last Sunday? It was about forgiveness. You need to forgive yourself."

She studied him for a moment. "You know, it makes sense to me now. *You* make sense to me."

"What are you talking about?"

"You have been so focused on setting yourself apart from your past, you became this stiff, by-the-Bible minister with no room to be yourself. Maybe you're afraid that if you let your guard down, you'll feel the pain of what happened. You went from being this human being to becoming a robot."

"A robot. Is that how you really see me?" Wade asked in a low, tormented voice.

"There was a time I felt that way," Pearl confessed. "But not anymore."

"The guilt of what happened has been hard to live with," Wade stated. "I kept thinking that if I could become this upstanding man…" He shook his head. "I have so much regret for the choices I made. I know God's forgiven me. My mother…" He let the word die on his lips.

"Have you ever tried to contact your mother?"

Wade nodded. "I called every now and then over the years. She would always hang up when she heard my voice."

"I'm so sorry." Pearl felt him shudder as he drew in a sharp breath.

"It's the consequences of my actions, Pearl. My sins."

After a moment, Pearl told Wade, "I don't think you should give up on your mother. In fact, why don't you call her now? Wish her a happy Thanksgiving."

He sighed, then gave a resigned shrug. "She won't talk to me."

"Call her, Wade," Pearl urged. "People can change over the years. You're proof of that."

"I don't know, Pearl. I'll pray about it."

"She's your mother. You can't just give up on her."

"Even though she gave up on me?"

"She was grieving, Wade. Trust me when I tell you that she's not only been grieving for your brother. She's been grieving for you, too."

Wade wasn't so sure. "I was grieving, too. I needed her, Pearl. After losing my dad and Jeff, I needed my mom desperately."

Her eyes were wet with tears. "I can't imagine what you must have gone through. If I didn't have my family, I don't know what I'd do. Wade, I'm so sorry."

"I try not to dwell on the negative. I'm thankful for Uncle Harold and Aunt Ivy. I would've been on the streets otherwise."

"Wade, don't you see? You made the choice to leave the gang. You chose not to let that gang-banger dic. You chose life. Sweetheart, you made the right choices. But now you need to live. You can't hide behind your sermons and the church." She smiled gently. "Do you want me to be there with you when you call your mother?"

"I never said I was going to call her."

"You will because it's the right thing to do. Wade, you, of all people, should know the God you serve."

"It's been my prayer for so long to be reunited with my mother."

"Trust Him and don't give up. Call your mom. I'll be right by your side."

Wade shook his head. "I need to do this alone. I hope you understand."

Pearl nodded. "I do."

She shivered. "It's cold out here. Are you ready to go back in the house?"

"I am."

"Good," Pearl uttered. "C'mon. I'm ready to tear into dessert."

"I still have to finish my dinner."

"Just skip it. We usually eat throughout the day, anyway."

Wade embraced her once they were standing on the porch. "Pearl Lockhart, I love you. I was afraid that once you knew about my past you'd want nothing to do with me."

"I know your heart, Wade. That's what's important. I'm not so naive that I don't realize we sometimes have to go through stuff to become the person we're meant to be. We make bad choices from time to time. Lord knows I've made my share. It's called life. We just can't stop living, though. We learn from our mistakes and move forward."

Crushing her to him, he pressed his mouth to

hers. Pearl kissed him back, lingering, savoring every moment.

"Ready to move forward?" Pearl asked before opening the front door.

Wade nodded. "I'm ready."

Grinning, she responded, "Okay, let's start with the white-chocolate bread pudding I made. You're going to want to marry me after you taste it."

"You really think it's *that* good?"

Laughing, she gently elbowed him.

Wade parked the car. "Despite my actions earlier, I really did have a good time today with your family. It's quite evident how close you and your sisters are. I think that's wonderful. I'd like to think that Jeff and I would've been like you and your sisters."

"We're a family…" The words died on her lips as Pearl realized what she'd said. "Wade, honey, I'm sorry. I didn't mean—"

He cut her off by saying, "It's okay."

Wade got out of the car, walked around to the other side and opened the door for Pearl.

She hugged him. "I love you, Wade."

"I love you, too."

He escorted her to the entrance of her building.

"You don't have to walk me up to the apartment," Pearl told him. "Go on home so that you can call your mom before it gets too late."

"I'll call you, no matter what happens."

"I'll be waiting. I don't care how late it is. I want you to call me and tell me how it went. Wade, you don't have to deal with this alone. Not anymore."

He nodded.

Pearl walked into her apartment, locking the door behind her. "Lord, please restore Wade's relationship with his mother. He needs her. He needs her love and he desperately needs her forgiveness. Maybe then, he'll be able to forgive himself."

Wade strode over to the phone when he walked into his house. He was touched by Pearl's offer to come over for moral support. However, Wade decided this was something he preferred to deal with alone.

"She not going to talk to me," he whispered. "I don't need to call and upset her."

Not wanting to deal with more rejection, Wade abandoned the idea of calling his mother. He went into the den and turned on the television.

His eyes kept straying back to the telephone. Pearl's words echoed around in his head. *She's right,* he decided. *My mother may have given up on me, but I won't give up on her.*

Wade picked up the phone and dialed.

"Hello."

"Mom, I...I just called to wish you a happy Thanksgiving." Wade waited for her to slam the phone down in his ear.

She didn't, but she didn't say anything, either.

"It's me. I... Mom, I'm sorry." The words suddenly came out in a rush. "I never meant for Jeff to get hurt. I'm so sorry."

Wade's words were met with silence.

His throat ached with defeat. "I hope one day you'll be able to forgive me. I love you and I miss you so much." Tears welled up and spilled out of his eyes. "Mom, please forgive me. I need your forgiveness."

Wade heard something that sounded like sobbing. His own tears rolled down his cheeks. Calling his mother had been a bad idea.

"I didn't mean to upset you. I just wanted to wish you a happy Thanksgiving and to apologize."

"Wade—"

The sound of his name rolling off her lips sent a wave of shock through him. "Yes, ma'am?"

"I'm so sorry. I'm so sorry for the way I've treated you. Son, I love you so much."

Wade could hardly believe what he was hearing. "Mama, can you ever forgive me?"

"I should be the one asking for forgiveness. I treated you so badly all these years. Just so caught up in my grief. Baby, I'm sorry."

"I love you, Mama."

"Harold kept me posted on how well you were doing. I'm so proud of you, Wade."

"I wanted to change my life. Be the man that Dad wanted me to become. I just hate that it took Jeff dying to get me to see the error of my ways. I think about him all the time."

"I do, too," his mother stated. "You stayed on my mind, too, Wade. I was just too consumed with my anger and grief."

"Mama, I understand. You'd lost your husband and then your son."

"I lost my husband and both my sons—that's the way I saw it. Wade, I'm so glad you called. I know what Harold and Ivy have told me, but why don't you tell me how you've been?"

"I've been doing okay, outside of missing you,

Dad and Jeff. I have been resting in the Lord and seeking His face. It's only because of Him that I've made it this far."

"It's so good to hear your voice."

Smiling, Wade responded, "Yours, too."

"Is there anyone special in your life?"

"I've met someone. Her name is Pearl Lockhart and I'm in love with her."

"That's wonderful, son. I'm happy for you."

"You'd like her, Mama."

She laughed. "I'm not so sure I'm willing to share you. I just got you back."

Wade and his mother stayed on the phone for almost two hours.

After getting her to agree to a short visit, Wade ended the call, feeling happier than he'd ever been in the past ten years.

Wade went into his bedroom and fell to his knees, thanking God for allowing him a second chance with his mother.

Chapter 17

Pearl paced back and forth across the living-room floor. Wade hadn't called her yet, so she didn't know if he'd spoken to his mother.

What if she hung up on him again? Pearl worried that Wade wouldn't be able to recover from another rejection. She worried that the advice she'd given him was wrong. "Lord, what have I done?"

"You okay?" Paige asked upon entering the apartment. "You look like you're fretting about something."

"Paige, I might have given Wade some bad advice. I'm afraid it might make things worse for him."

Without betraying Wade's confidence and revealing his personal story, Pearl told her cousin about his estrangement from his mother, and about the phone call.

Her own telephone rang, cutting her off.

"I hope that's Wade." Pearl rushed over to the phone, picking it up on the third ring. "How did it go?"

"I spoke with my mother," Wade answered on the other end of the phone. "We actually had a good conversation."

"Thank You, Jesus!" Pearl shouted.

Wade chuckled. "That's exactly what I said when I hung up. Sweetheart, I can't describe what I'm feeling right now. I feel like a huge weight has been lifted off me."

"I'm so happy for you."

"I feel pretty good about things myself."

"I'm so glad you listened to me. You and your mother have been apart far too long."

"It's funny you should say that, sweetheart. As a matter of fact, I'm flying my mom to Detroit this weekend. She's arriving tomorrow afternoon. We didn't want another day to go by without seeing each other."

"What a wonderful blessing," Pearl murmured. "I'm so happy for you, Wade."

"This feels good."

"I'm sure." Pearl swiped at a tear. She could hear the happiness in Wade's voice and her heart leapt with joy. "Sweetheart, I have to work the morning shift tomorrow, but if you don't mind, I'd like to go with you to the airport."

"Great. I want you to be there with me. I can't wait for the two of you to meet. I already told my mom that she's going to love you."

Pearl sat quietly listening as Wade talked about old memories, when his father was alive and they were still a family.

"This has been some Thanksgiving, huh? Opal and D'marcus getting engaged, you and your mother reuniting."

"What about us?" Wade questioned. "Letting your family know that we're a couple."

"That, too. We have a lot to be thankful for."

"Amen," Wade murmured.

Pearl rode the wave of sleeplessness back and forth. She kept waking up every hour, it seemed.

Finally she gave up on the idea of sleeping and reached for her laptop, taking it off the nightstand and placing it in bed with her.

As if following some unseen guide, Pearl found herself on the Internet, searching the archives of Chicago newspapers. She was looking for any information on Jeff Kendrick's death.

Why now, when Wade and his mother were reuniting? Still, Wade was in pain because of his brother's death. That pain probably stemmed from Wade's guilt that he didn't die that day.

Pearl found an article on the shooting and began to read.

According to an eyewitness account, corroborated by the injured gang member, Jeff pushed Wade out of the way.

"He tried to save him," Pearl murmured. "Jeff died saving his brother's life. Wade never told me."

Now she had a better understanding of why Wade blamed himself. He had allowed his brother to join the gang and then Jeff ended up saving his life.

What an awesome testimony, Pearl realized. If only Wade could see it himself. While what happened to his brother was tragic, Wade's turning to the Lord was the gift in all this.

Pearl hoped that Wade would one day be able to share his experiences with the youth at church—they needed to hear his testimony. They would listen to him.

"Give him the strength he needs," she prayed. "Wade needs to forgive himself and only You can help him."

Pearl stopped by the church offices the next day before her shift at Milton's.

"Is Pastor expecting you?" asked Barbara, who began her interrogation of Pearl the moment she walked into the administration building requesting to see Wade.

"I told him I might be stopping by," Pearl replied. "I spoke with him earlier."

"What do you need to see him about?"

Instead of answering her question, Pearl posed one of her own. "Is Pastor here?" She knew that Barbara had Wade picked out for her niece.

Pearl was positive that Wade would never be interested in someone like Marnie, who dressed too suggestively and boldly flaunted her sexuality.

"The Pastor is a busy man, Pearl. He don't have no time for no foolishness. I've known you since you were a little girl, so I'm just offering you a tiny piece of advice. Pray and ask God to send you a husband. You don't have to go running down the Pastor."

"I'm not here for 'foolishness' as you put it," Pearl replied as calmly as she could. "Sister Barbara, I know that you've been hoping that Marnie would catch Pastor's eye but there's one thing you haven't considered."

"And what's that?" Barbara huffed, her hands on her hips.

"Pastor Kendrick has a mind of his own. He is the one who decides whom he allows into his life. Why don't you ask him if he's interested in your niece?"

Barbara didn't respond.

Pearl continued. "He's not some brainless man who will marry the first girl thrown at him. You should take your own advice. Let Pastor pick the woman he wants to be with. I'm sure he doesn't need any help from you."

"Humph," Barbara grunted. "You seem to be the authority on Pastor."

Pearl held her temper in check. "I'm not saying that at all. There is something you need to know, Sister Barbara. Wade and I are dating."

"Excuse me?"

"We're seeing each other." Pearl folded her arms across her chest. "He's already chosen someone."

"I don't believe it."

"Just ask him. He'll tell you."

Wade walked out into the waiting area, interrupting their conversation. "Pearl, I've been expecting you."

Barbara's eyes bounced from Pearl's face to Wade's, trying to examine their expressions.

"Is something wrong?" Wade inquired.

"I was just telling Sister Barbara our news," Pearl stated with a grin.

"You always were a fast tail," Barbara uttered. "Pastor, I hope you know what you doing."

Wade's eyes traveled to Pearl's. "Why don't we talk in my office?"

Pearl agreed, following him down the hall.

"We should leave the door open," Wade whispered.

"No problem." She pulled a CD out of her purse. "I wanted you to listen to this and tell me what you think. It's the song I've been working on. I finished it."

"I'm sure I'm going to love it."

Their eyes met and held, locked in a heated gaze.

Pearl broke the look. "I—I need to get to Milton's. My shift starts in half an hour. I just stopped by to say hello and give you the CD."

"I'm going to see you in a few hours. You're still going to the airport with me, right?"

"Okay, the truth is that I just wanted to see your handsome face," Pearl confessed. "I couldn't wait until later."

"I'm glad you stopped by."

Grinning, she took Wade by the hand. "Walk me out to my car?"

He led her out of his office. Pearl wasn't surprised to find Barbara hovering nearby pretending to be busy.

"Have a good day, Sister Barbara," Pearl said with a smile.

Barbara threw up a hand before stalking off, muttering beneath her breath.

Wade and Pearl waited until they were outside the building before breaking into laughter.

"Your secretary is so upset with me. She really wants you and Marnie together."

"I know, but Marnie and I actually had a conversation. She knew that we never stood a chance."

"Oh, really?"

Wade nodded. "I made it clear that I wasn't interested."

"I hope you weren't quite so blunt. You did let her down easy, didn't you?"

"She asked me a direct question and I gave her a straight answer."

Pearl didn't respond. She seemed preoccupied.

Kissing her on the cheek, Wade inquired, "What are you thinking about?"

Pearl glanced over at Wade. "I was just thinking that you should share your story with the boys at the church. You could really reach them if you do."

Wade shook his head. "I've already tried that."

They walked over to his car and sat inside. "You told them you were involved in a gang?"

"No, not exactly."

"Sweetheart, those kids see you the way I used to—as a stuffy ol' pastor who is beyond reproach. They figure you can't relate to what they're going through."

"I don't know if I can share that part of my past with them, with anyone. It was hard enough to tell you that my brother died because I was a coward. I broke a promise to my mother and I only thought about saving my own skin. I didn't look out for Jeff or T-Bone. I let them both down."

"Wade, there is another way to look at this," Pearl pointed out. "Your brother died saving your life. He saved you."

"What are you talking about?"

"Jeff jumped in front of you. He loved you so much that he died protecting you."

"How do you know this?"

"Wade, you didn't know?" Pearl paused for a moment then began again. "I thought you knew but were just feeling guilty about it. I did some re-search. There was an eyewitness and the other guy who was shot. They both told the police that your brother shoved you out of the way and got caught in the crossfire."

Memories of that day instantly assailed Wade. He remembered hanging out with his boys on that day long ago. He recalled walking down the street laughing and talking with Jeff and T-Bone.

In his mind, Wade saw the slow, deliberate ap-proach of a black car coming down the street. He stiffened from the memory, recalling the ominous feeling he felt as the car neared.

Wade remembered reaching for Jeff as his instincts drove him to seek safety, but in a matter of seconds, he felt himself being shoved to the ground. He could hear himself yelling... screaming for Jeff to take cover.

His words were drowned out by the loud cracking sound of rapid gunfire. Wade remembered covering his ears to block out the sound.

When it was over, Jeff and T-Bone lay on the sidewalk bleeding. Wade held Jeff in his arms until the paramedics arrived. T-Bone ended up paralyzed from the waist down, while his brother died en route to the hospital.

"Wade, are you all right?"

Pearl's voice summoned him out of the past. "What did you say?"

"I asked if you were okay."

"I remember everything," Wade uttered. "I remember what happened the day Jeff died. It was never real clear in the past. All this time..."

"Wade, you can choose to blame yourself and live in the past or cherish the memory of a brother who loved you so much that he gave up his own life for yours. Honor him by helping other youth. Keep them from being seduced into the gang life."

Chapter 18

Pearl eyed the clock. Wade would be picking her up for the airport in ten minutes.

"We're going to get a quick bite to eat and stop by the florist before we head to the airport," Pearl told her cousin. "I probably won't be back until after eight tonight."

"You're not gonna hang out with Wade and his mother?"

Pearl shook her head. "I think they need some quality time together. This will be the first time he's seen her in ten years."

"I'm really happy for him. When you get back here, I want you to tell me every single tearjerking moment. Don't forget to take tissue with you—enough for you and Wade."

Pearl laughed. "You're crazy."

"This is a reunion, Pearl. I'm tearing up just thinking about it." Paige wiped at her eyes.

Wade's arrival curtailed their conversation.

"Are you nervous?" Pearl asked him as soon as they stepped on the elevator.

"A little," he confessed. "The last time I saw my mother was at the cemetery and she was so angry."

"She was grieving, sweetie. People grieve in different ways. Just remember that she loves you. She's on a plane right now because she wants to see you, Wade."

"I know. She was hurt. I hurt her by not protecting my brother. I understand it and I accept responsibility." Wade stole a peek at Pearl. "I've made peace with my past."

"I bet your mother is just as nervous about seeing you again."

"It's been a long time. I've missed her so much."

"I'm sure she missed you, too."

Wade grew silent as they neared the airport.

Pearl reached over and took his hand. "It's going to be okay."

He nodded but didn't respond. Wade parked the car. "Her plane should be arriving in about ten minutes."

Pearl gave him a reassuring hug before they walked inside the terminal baggage-claim area.

"Let me hold the flowers. You're going to squeeze the life out of them."

Wade gave her a tiny smile. "Thanks."

Pearl led him over to some empty chairs. "Sit down, sweetheart. We can't have you passing out. I don't think your mom should see you all laid out on the floor." Grinning, she added, "It's just not the best impression."

Wade's breath caught in his throat when he recognized his mother's thin frame as she walked down the escalator. Her hair was peppered with gray but otherwise she still looked the same. Time had been kind to her over the years.

"There she is," he whispered to Pearl. "Arlene Kendrick. My mother."

Arlene's eyes traveled the area, searching.

"Mom," he called out.

Wade strolled across the floor, rushing to meet his mother. He greeted his mother with a hug. "I'm so glad to see you," he whispered in her ear. "God has answered my prayers."

"Oh, baby," she murmured, her voice filled with tears. "I've missed you so much."

Wade placed an arm around Pearl. "Mom, I want you to meet a very special person. This is Pearl Lockhart."

"Is this your girlfriend?"

Smiling, Wade nodded. "Yes. This is my girlfriend. She's the one I was telling you about on the telephone."

"It's such a pleasure to meet you, Mrs. Kendrick."

She embraced Pearl. "I'm so happy to meet you."

Five minutes later, the luggage was placed in the trunk and everyone was seated in the car.

"How was your flight?" Wade asked his mother while driving away from the airport.

"Good. I think I slept the entire hour I was on the flight." She chuckled. "I'm so excited to be here."

"Uncle Harold and Aunt Ivy invited us over for dinner tomorrow night," Wade announced. "They want you to come, too, Pearl."

"I work the afternoon shift so I should be off in time."

She reached over and squeezed his hand. When Wade glanced over at her, Pearl winked.

Words couldn't describe what he was feeling at the moment. Wade was surrounded by the two most important women in his life. His mother and Pearl had hit it off immediately and were fast becoming friends.

He smiled as he listened to them chat about shopping and where to find the best sales. It was Black Friday and his mother had spent most of her day catching sales.

"I've already got all of my Christmas shopping done," she was saying. "This is the first year I'm actually looking forward to Christmas."

"Same here, Mom." Wade glanced over at Pearl. "All I've wanted is to share my life with you. God has not only answered that prayer but he has blessed me with Pearl."

The fashion show and luncheon on Saturday was a success, much to Pearl's relief.

"So what did you think?" she asked Wade. "Still questioning my sense of style?"

"I'm impressed, Pearl. I should've trusted you from the very beginning."

"Yeah. You should have, but it's okay. I thought about our initial conversation about clothing and I kept that in mind when selecting the clothes. I mainly wanted to give the teens some ideas on how to be fashionable without having to show all of their goodies."

"You did a wonderful job, Pearl."

"Thank you for saying that. I really appreciate it."

Arlene walked over to them with Harold and Ivy. She embraced Pearl saying, "You did a beautiful job putting all this together. And that song you sang was beautiful. Just beautiful."

"Thank you," Pearl murmured. She hugged Harold and Ivy. "How was the food?"

"Delicious," they said in unison.

Pearl glanced over at Wade. "You haven't said anything. Did *you* like the food? I tried a new caterer this year. One of the sisters in the church started a business and I wanted to help her out."

"I enjoyed it."

"I'm glad to hear that because she's going to be catering our church anniversary dinner." Pearl spotted her sisters. "Excuse me, please. I need to catch my sisters before they leave. I'll be right back."

Pearl walked over to where Opal, Ruby and Amber were sitting. "Did y'all like the show?"

Ruby nodded. "Your friend has some wonderful designs. Congratulations, Pearl. You did well."

Opal agreed.

"I'm thinking about ordering the entire line," Amber stated. "I loved everything."

"Looks like Pastor's family likes you," Opal said. "I talked to his mother a little bit before the fashion show. She thinks the world of you."

"Mrs. Kendrick is a sweetheart. I'm so glad she and Wade have been able to spend this time together."

"He's changed since the two of you got together," Amber commented. "I like this Wade Kendrick so much better. See what love can do for a person."

Pearl eyed her baby sister. "Amber, I hope you don't think you can change Dashuan Kennedy."

"Let's not ruin everything," Opal interjected. "We'll discuss that situation later."

"No discussion needed," Amber stated. "I'm grown. I can make my own choices."

Ruby was the first to rise. "I hate to rush off

but I have some work I need to finish. Great job, Pearl."

Opal and Amber followed suit.

Pearl walked her sisters to the door, then glanced around the room, looking for Wade.

Justine Raymond walked up to her. "I thought you told me you weren't interested in Pastor. I heard Sister Barbara over there saying that the two of you are a couple now."

"We are," Pearl confirmed. "But I didn't deliberately set out to snare Wade. Our relationship just happened."

"Do you love him?"

Pearl met Justine's gaze straight on. "Yeah, I do."

"And he feels the same way about you?"

Pearl nodded. "Yes."

Justine let out a small sigh. "I can't say I'm not disappointed, but I'm happy it's you and not some hoochie. Well, I'll see you later. I see a man over there I need to meet. You got your man and I need to get mine."

"Good luck with that."

Pearl found Wade sitting at the table with his mother and the Greens. She went over and joined them.

"Did your sisters leave?" Wade asked.

"Yeah."

Barbara and Marnie walked by the table, looking as if they smelled something bad.

"What's wrong with them?" Arlene asked in a low voice.

"Barbara's the church secretary," Wade explained. "And she's just a little disappointed that I didn't choose her niece."

Glancing over her shoulder to get another look at the two women, Arlene muttered, "I see."

Ivy laughed. "I'm sure Pearl has made a lot of enemies here at Lakeview since hooking up with Wade."

"Wade's the man over here," Pearl stated with a grin.

"Behave," Wade told her with a wink. He stood up. "I need to talk to Yolanda. I want to check on Tyson."

"I can't wait for you to hear Wade preach, Mrs. Kendrick," Pearl said after he'd left the table. "He does a wonderful job."

"I'm so proud of him. My mother told me the day Wade was born that he was destined to be a preacher."

"He's a good man."

"Yes, he is." Arlene reached over, taking Pearl's hand. "You make him happy."

"He makes me happy, too."

"You're good for each other," Ivy interjected. "I can see a big difference in Wade."

"What are you all talking about?" Wade inquired when he returned, reclaiming his seat beside Pearl.

"You," she responded. "Surely you didn't expect us to talk about anything else. Sweetheart, it's all about you."

Arlene and Ivy chuckled while Harold said, "You're certainly going to have your hands full with her."

Wade laughed. "Yes, I am, but I'm up to the challenge."

Chapter 19

"Mom, there's something I need to do this morning," Wade announced over breakfast. "I've been wrestling with this for a while and I know this is what God wants me to do. I'm just not sure how you're going to feel about it."

"What is it, son?"

"I need to talk about what happened. Some of the kids in my church are running with gang members. I don't want them to make the same mistake I made. I don't want to let another teen go down like Jeff. If I don't say something—"

"Son, you've got to do it," Arlene said, cutting him off. She sat her coffee cup down on the table. "Wade, you have to tell them. Don't worry about me. I'll be fine. Maybe if they hear about Jeff, it'll save some child's life."

"I missed you so much, Mom."

"I missed you, too. I hope that you can forgive me, Wade. I never should've kicked you out of my life like that. You were a child." Arlene took a sip of her coffee. "I used to have these dreams of your father right after he died. We would be in a park somewhere. He never said a word, just smiled the entire time we were together. Even the night Jeff was gone he came to me. We didn't walk this time. We just sat on one of the benches and held each other while we cried. After the funeral, the dreams changed. Larry would just give me this sad, hurtful look. We didn't take walks, just sat on that bench not looking at each another."

Arlene suddenly broke into a smile. "Until last night."

"What happened last night?"

"This time when Larry met me in the park, he had Jeff with him. They were both smiling." Arlene's eyes filled with tears. "I'm sure you think this is strange or just my way of dealing with my loss. Maybe it is, but I know that Larry wasn't pleased with me for the way I treated you. Neither was Jeff."

"I don't think it's strange at all. I used to dream about Dad and Jeff, too. I was feeling so much guilt, I just wanted the dreams to go away. I started taking medication to help me sleep. Now I can't sleep without it."

"Oh, son…"

"It's not your fault, Mom. This is about me and not being able to forgive myself. God and I had a long talk last night and He led me to His Word. I have to give my testimony this morning. I have to become more involved with the youth in the community. I can't keep walking around like the past never happened."

"I'm so proud of you, Wade."

He smiled. Wade had waited a long time to hear those words.

"Your dad and Jeff would be so proud of you, too."

When they finished eating, Wade placed the dishes into the dishwasher. He went to his bedroom to get dressed for church.

Arlene met him in the living room twenty minutes later. "Is Lakeview a big church?"

"I guess you might say that. It's much bigger than our church back home."

"Wade, it's been such a blessing to be here with you this weekend. I regret so much that I let all this time go by. I—"

He held up his hand, cutting her off. "Mom, the past is the past. We have now. This is what's important."

Fifteen minutes later, Wade pulled into the parking lot of Lakeview Baptist Church.

"Oh, my, this *is* a big church," Arlene murmured. "Does the congregation like you?"

"I think so," Wade responded. "The only person I ever really had a problem with was Pearl."

"Pearl?"

He laughed. "I'll tell you about it after the service."

Arlene left Wade in his office to spend some time alone in prayer. He prayed for strength and courage for what was in his heart.

He made his way to the sanctuary and traveled among the congregation, looking for Pearl. She and her sisters were sitting with his mother. He noted D'marcus Armstrong had joined them this morning. Wade gave him a slight nod.

After the choir sang their third song, Wade stood up to speak.

"This Sunday I want to talk to the youth especially," Wade announced to the congregation. "Our kids are in crisis. If we're not careful, we will find them on the cusp of being involved in gangs or drug addiction and ending up in prison."

He paused for a few minutes, gathering his thoughts.

"I'd like to share something from my past. You see, I know what I'm talking about. Church, I'm not coming to you with something that I've read or seen on television. I've lived it."

Wade's eyes traveled to his mother, who gave him a smile of encouragement. She put her hand to her lips, blowing him a kiss.

"I am an ex-gang affiliate," Wade announced. "When I was fifteen years old, I joined a gang called the Chicago Kings."

A low murmur of surprise moved throughout the congregation. They never expected to hear this admission, but Wade knew he had to continue.

"Young people, I knew some guys who didn't mind the daily bullets that never pierced their flesh somehow. Back then my brothers didn't care when someone held a gun to their head and their soul ached. The reason they didn't care was because they had no purpose, no hope. They weren't afraid of dying. They *wanted* to die because to them death was a man's way out. Death was better than the life they were living."

Wade paused long enough to let his words sink in. "We used to suit up with loaded weapons and nothing to lose on Friday and Saturday nights in search of mischief and house parties. Add alcohol to the equation, and only God knows what could happen. In a way, we were already dead. Gang members are already dead. Today I am on a mission to awaken the dead."

Wade's eyes traveled to Pearl. She smiled at him as a show of support.

"My world came crashing down around me when my brother Jeff was killed. My mother made me promise to look out for him and even though I told her that I would, I didn't stop him from joining the gang." Tears formed in his eyes. "He wanted to be like me. The day he was killed all I could think about was that I should have been the one to die. Jeff died because he pushed me out of the way. He was looking out for me even though I hadn't looked out for him."

Wade managed to finish his sermon without

breaking down in front of the congregation. He called the youth up to the front of the church.

"We're going to pray for our young people," he stated. "We're going to awaken the dead."

"Wade, you did a wonderful job this morning," Pearl complimented as they walked down the hallway toward his office. "I think you really captured the attention of the teens when you were talking. I looked around and they were all listening to you."

"You think so?"

She nodded. "They really needed to hear your testimony, Wade. I'm so glad you shared your story with them. I'm proud of you."

"I hope I was able to reach them. I don't want another teen to ever go through what I experienced."

"I believe you did reach them."

"Pastor… Oh!" Marnie stopped short when she saw Pearl. "I didn't know you had someone in here."

"Did you need something?"

"I just wanted to commend you on the talk you gave this morning. What an awesome testimony."

Pearl nodded in agreement.

"Thank you for your kind words. I appreciate it."

"That's all I wanted to say." Marnie glanced

over at Pearl. "Enjoy the rest of your day." She turned to leave but paused long enough to add, "I never thought I'd say this, but you two make a beautiful couple."

When Marnie was gone, Pearl eyed Wade. "Wow. I never thought we'd hear those words coming out of her mouth."

He smiled. "She's right. We make a good couple."

"Beautiful, sweetheart. She said we're a beautiful couple. Get it right."

"We'd better get going. Mom's waiting on us."

"Ruby and Opal are taking good care of her, I'm sure."

"I didn't see Amber in church this morning."

"That's because she wasn't here. She went out with that jerk Dashuan last night and didn't get in until early this morning. I don't know why that girl has to be so hardheaded. Even D'marcus has warned her against seeing Dashuan. Amber just won't listen."

"She's an adult, honey."

"I know. It's just that she's also my sister and—"

"You Lockharts stick together," Wade finished for her.

When they walked outside, Wade spotted Tyson standing with a young man who looked vaguely familiar. Wade strolled toward them. "G-Dog?"

The boy nodded. "It's me," he said sheepishly. "Tyson asked me to come to church with him this morning. I thought it was whack, but I came anyway. I liked your sermon."

G-Dog had traded his long white shirt and oversized jeans for a pair of corduroy pants, a sweater and a leather jacket. Instead of the bandana, he wore a black wool cap.

"I'm glad you decided to join us," Wade told him.

"Mom said the only way G-Dog and I could hang was if he came to church with me," Tyson explained.

"Does that mean we'll be seeing you again?"

G-Dog gave a slight nod. "I'll be back, Pastor."

"Miss Pearl, you should hear G-Dog sing," Tyson stated with a grin. "He can blow. He raps, too."

Pearl glanced over at the teen. "Really?"

"I ain't singing in no choir." G-Dog shook his head. "I said I'd come to church with you but singing…I ain't wit that."

"We're not going to push you to do anything you don't want to do," Wade assured him. "But, G-Dog, if you ever feel like you need to talk about anything, I want you to know my door is always open."

"You was really a member of the Chicago Kings? I heard about those dudes. Man, they ain't no joke."

He nodded. "I still have the tattoo to prove it. I've had laser surgery to remove most of it, but just like the choices we make, there are always remnants left."

D'marcus and Opal walked over to where they were standing. Pearl introduced them to G-Dog.

"Do you boys like basketball?" D'marcus asked.

They both nodded.

"I'll give Pastor Wade some tickets to the game on Wednesday. If you're interested in going, I'm sure he'll be more than happy to speak with your parents."

"For real?" G-Dog asked.

Wade nodded. "I'll pick you up and bring you home."

He gave D'marcus a grateful smile.

G-Dog was suspicious. "So what we got to do for the tickets?"

"Nothing," Wade answered. "However, there is one rule. No gang gear."

"I'm not in a gang, Pastor. My brother is and I wanted to be a member of the Disciples but…" He paused. "I don't wanna die. My brother says I'm nothin' but a punk."

"Your brother is wrong," Pearl interjected. "I think you're very brave for admitting your fears and making the right choice. We'll pray that your brother will find the courage to do the same. By the way, what's your real name? I don't like calling you G-Dog."

"Gerald," he uttered.

Giving him a smile, Pearl asked, "Do you mind if I call you Gerald?"

He smiled back and said, "No."

Tyson hit his friend on the arm. "We got to go. Mom's already in the car." To Wade he asked, "You really gonna talk to her about the game?"

He nodded. "I'll call her tonight."

G-Dog hesitated. "I need to give you my phone number so you can talk to my mom, too."

When the boys were gone, Wade told D'marcus, "I really appreciate you donating those tickets. I need to find a way to reach them and maybe this is the way to do it."

Early the next morning, Pearl woke up to the sound of the telephone ringing.

It was Opal.

"You are not going to believe this," she began. "Amber's in Los Angeles with Dashuan Kennedy."

Pearl shot straight up in bed. "What? Are you sure?"

"Yeah. She left with him."

"That girl has lost her mind," Pearl fussed. "I don't know what she's thinking."

"This is crazy."

Sighing with resignation, Pearl climbed out of bed. "Amber's not a child anymore. We can't lock her in her room or anything. She's on her own."

"She's our sister. Ruby's calling Luther to see if he has any suggestions. We all know Dashuan's bad news. We have to be prepared to bring Amber home."

Upset, Pearl called Wade next.

"You're not going to believe this," she began. "Amber went to Los Angeles with Dashuan Kennedy."

"She did what?"

"She ran off to L.A. Can you believe that? Ruby's calling Luther right now. We're going to go get her."

"Honey, I know how much you care about Amber, but this is her life. She's an adult and you can't force her to come home until she's ready. I know this is hard for you to hear but it's the truth."

Pearl tossed a pillow across her room. "I know you're right, Wade. Life is about the choices we make and learning to live with the consequences." She released a long sigh. "I'm so glad to have you in my life, Wade."

"Honey, we can handle anything life throws at us as long as we're together. You are the love of my life, Pearl, and I thank God for you."

"Same here," Pearl murmured with a soft chuckle. "I never thought in a million years that I'd be the preacher's woman. But I'm loving every minute of it."

* * * * *

Watch for the next exciting book
in Kimani Romance's
THE LOCKHARTS—THREE WEDDINGS
& A REUNION
For four sassy sisters,
romance changes everything!
HIS HOLIDAY BRIDE
by
Elaine Overton
Available in October 2007

Grown and sultry...

CANDICE POARCH

As a girl, Jasmine wanted Drake desperately, but
Drake considered his best friend's baby sister
completely off-limits. Now Jasmine is all grown up,
and goes to work for Drake, and he's stunned by the
explosive desire he feels for her. Even though she still
has way too much attitude, Drake finds himself
unable to resist the sassy, sexy beauty....

*Available the first week of September
wherever books are sold.*

The follow-up to *Sweet Surrender*
and *Here and Now...*

Straight to the Heart

Bestselling author

MICHELLE MONKOU

Fearful that her unsavory past is about to be exposed,
hip-hop diva Stacy Watts dates clean-cut Omar Masterson
to save her new image. But their playacting backfires
when their mutual attraction starts to burn out of control!
Now Stacy must fight to keep the secrets of her past
from destroying her future with Omar.

*Available the first week of September
wherever books are sold.*

KIMANI™
ROMANCE

www.kimanipress.com

He was the first man to touch her soul...

SOUL Caress

Favorite author

KIM SHAW

When privileged Kennedy Daniels loses her sight, hospital orderly Malik Crawford helps heal her wounds and awaken her desire. But they come from different worlds, so unless Kennedy's willing to defy her prominent family, a future between them is impossible.

Available the first week of September wherever books are sold.

KIMANI™
ROMANCE

Essence bestselling author

DONNA

She's ready for her close-up...

Moments Like This

Part of the Romance in the Spotlight series

Actress and model Dominique Laws has been living the
Hollywood dream—fame, fortune, a handsome husband—
but lately good roles have been scarce. Then she learns
that her business-manager husband has been cheating
on her personally and financially. Suddenly, she's down
and out in Beverly Hills. But a chance meeting with a
Denzel-fine filmmaker may offer the role of a lifetime....

**Available the first week of September,
wherever books are sold.**

ARABESQUE®

www.kimanipress.com

KPDH0190907

National bestselling author

KIM LOUISE

Ever Wonderful

When his truck hits Ariana Macleod's prized Angus,
Braxton Ambrose goes to work on her ranch to
repay her. Handsome Brax's presence feels very
welcome to Ariana—especially when their mutual
attraction explodes into a sizzling affair. Brax isn't the
settling-down type, but when tragedy strikes, he's
determined to convince Ariana that he'll be
with her for the long haul.

"Heartbreaking, heartwarming and downright funny,
this story will totally captivate any reader from
beginning to end."
—*Romantic Times BOOKreviews* on
True Devotion

**Available the first week of September,
wherever books are sold.**

ARABESQUE®
www.kimanipress.com

KPKL0180907